# Dreamcatcher's Face

### Vernon Yoder

PublishAmerica
Baltimore

© 2006 by Vernon Yoder.
All rights reserved. No part of this book may be reproduced, stored in a retrieval system or transmitted in any form or by any means without the prior written permission of the publishers, except by a reviewer who may quote brief passages in a review to be printed in a newspaper, magazine or journal.

First printing

All characters appearing in this work are fictitious. Any resemblance to real persons, living or dead, is purely coincidental.

ISBN: 1-4241-4805-7
PUBLISHED BY PUBLISHAMERICA, LLLP
www.publishamerica.com
Baltimore

Printed in the United States of America

Dedicated to my grandmother Dorothy Yoder
and my father Carl Yoder,
both who taught be the value
of reading a good book.

# Chapter 1

The sweat rolled off of Roy Curtis' face as he put the last bale of hay from that load in place. It was close to one hundred degrees in the hayloft and there was absolutely no breeze moving in the old barn. The original bank barn had been built around the turn of the last century. A lighting strike in 1936 had reduced that structure to ashes and a new barn had been constructed on the old foundation by Roy's grandfather. Grandpa's barn, as Roy referred to it, was built in the typical bank barn design that was common in Northern Indiana. A huge loft area was constructed over a milking parlor and cattle loafing area. This loft was capable of holding about three thousand, fifty-pound, bales of hay and on more than one occasion in his life Roy had assisted in filling it and just as many times he had helped empty it as feed for the cattle that lived below. The old barn was still a good building, but hot and stuffy during the dog days of August. Climbing down the wooden ladder out of the loft Roy could feel the sweat soaked T-shirt cling to his well-muscled back. Skipping the last four rungs of the ladder, Curtis jumped onto the wooden floor of the barn. Turning he headed out the door as the three teenage boys who had been helping unload the hay pushed the wagon out the door.

Reaching for the water hydrant, Roy turned it on to let the water cool. Picking up the hose, he removed his old battered ball cap, and proceeded to drench his head with the cold well water. After rinsing his arms off, Curtis took a long drink before handing the hose off to one of the teens. He felt refreshed by the cold water and was ready for the next load of hay. As the owner of the farm, Roy didn't have to spend his summer weekends unloading hay, but he chose to anyway, as it helped to relieve stress and keep him in shape.

Roy walked over and sat in the shade of the old barn as he waited for the next wagon to be pulled inside. Sitting there he let his mind drift back to his high school days, when he had been one of the guys spending his summer days baling hay just trying to make enough money so he could call some girl up and go see a movie. Twenty-five years ago the Seven C Cattle Co., as the farm was called now, had only been a couple of hundred acres in size. Barely large enough to make ends meet let alone send an ambitious young man to college.

The birth of a very exceptional bull calf that one cold January night over twenty years ago had changed the farm and the way the Curtis's lived their lives. Midnight Ranger turned out to be one of the breed's best and had been named National Champion as a two-year-old at the American Royal Livestock Show in Kansas City. The money earned from the breeding fees and his calves had allowed the Seven C Cattle Co. to expand and Roy to go to college.

"Hey!" a voice hollered, knocking Roy's mind back to the present. "You gonna sit there all afternoon or are you gonna help? Maybe you're getting too old for this?" The farm manager, Justin Roberts, was getting out of his truck and heading up the bank of the barn with a large thermos.

"Too old? I can bury you any day unloading hay, Roberts," Curtis replied." What do you got in the jug?"

"Maria thought you might like some iced tea. So I told her that I would bring you some if you said please."

"Please, please, oh pretty please," Curtis begged like a little child wanting a piece of candy from his mother.

"OK, since you asked so nicely, catch." Roberts tossed the

thermos at him. Curtis caught the jug with ease, opened the spout, and let the ice-cold liquid pour down his throat.

"Thanks, I might be able to finish this last load. I am about whipped. Remember when we used to do this all day, go paint the town until two a.m., and then get up do it all over again?" Justin and Roy had grown up together as teenagers, traveling the country showing cattle, making hay, and chasing girls. The two had first met as high school freshmen, when they had both signed on with the Double Ace Ranch out of El Reno, Oklahoma, to groom cattle for the ranch's show string. They had worked together all that summer and started a friendship that continued to the present.

"Yeah, I remember," Justin said, "and you had better be able to do it again tonight. While I was at the house, Sara Mitchell called. She and Dave are having a cookout tonight and they insist that you come over. Maria said that you would be delighted."

"Someday I am going to fire that busybody of a housekeeper."

"Right, just after they open an ice skating rink in hell," Roberts laughed.

"OK so I can't fire her," Roy admitted," but I really hate it when she does that. I know Sara is going to have at least a half a dozen ladies there to parade me in front of. I just feel like I am at a job interview or a slab of meat at the butcher shop when she does that."

"She just doesn't like seeing you alone," Justin commented, "besides you never know, you might just get lucky."

"OK, OK, I give up," Roy conceded, as he signaled surrender with his hands. "Besides here comes the last wagon in from the field." Stiffly he pushed himself up off of the ground, picked up his old battered hat, slapped it against his leg, smashed it on top of his head, grabbed leather gloves and headed inside the barn to help. Justin headed back to the Ford pickup.

"Don't forget, seven o'clock at the Mitchell's house. Don't be late," Roberts ordered, "or Sara will beat knots on your head. Lisa and I will be there for you to hide behind if you can't fend off the women."

"Oh get out of here!" Curtis hollered as he climbed back up the ladder to the mow. "Start up that elevator, boys, it is Saturday night and we got things to do and places to go." With that the bales of hay started up the chain elevator to the loft.

"What to wear? What to wear?" Curtis muttered to himself as he stood looking in the closet. The temptation was to go to the cookout dressed like a slob so that the women would leave him alone, but he knew that would only incur Sara Mitchell's wrath and that is worse than any woman who might feel like chasing him. Sara's parties were always events of culture and she expected her guests to dress accordingly. Roy chose a pair of tan western cut trousers, blue oxford shirt, and a dark blue silk sports coat. Shedding the Turkish terry robe, Roy dressed quickly and carefully. He used to enjoy getting ready for parties, but that was when there had been a Mrs. Curtis.

Roy pulled his pant legs down over his brown calfskin boots, picked up his Stetson hat and then headed down the hall. Maria was in the kitchen washing some fresh vegetables that her husband, Henri, had brought in. Maria and Henri Gonzalez had been in the employ of the Curtis family for forty years as housekeeper and gardener-caretaker. Henri's horticultural skills were such that the gardens of the Seven C Cattle Co. were enjoyed and envied by people in the four adjacent counties. Maria was an excellent cook and could lay a spread that would stuff the hungriest young man around. The farm never had trouble getting high school boys to help with the nasty jobs; all Justin would have to do was to let it be known that the job included a meal and the boys would form a line to be hired.

"There is a pitcher of fresh tea in the refrigerator," Maria said without turning around. Roy took a big glass from the cupboard, filled it with ice, and poured the still warm tea into the glass. The ice crackled and popped as the warm liquid rushed over the cubes. Iced tea was Roy's favorite drink and Maria kept a pitcher made up year round.

" Thanks." Roy answered as he took a huge drink of the tea. Finishing the glass, Roy put the glass on the counter next to the sink where Maria was working. Sighing, he turned to head out the back door. Maria grabbed his arm and stopped him before he took the first step.

"I know you miss her and the boy, but it has been over ten years and you must get on with your life. Now get going before you are late and Sara Mitchell has a fit. Just go have fun. OK?"

"OK, Maria, I will try," Roy replied.

"Well try harder," was the motherly advice the elderly housekeeper gave. "And by the way, Mr. Curtis, you do look handsome. If I was twenty years younger...."

"That's enough, Maria. If Henri hears you talking like that he will chase me around the house with the hoe," Roy laughed and headed out the back door.

Roy crossed the lawn and opened the wooden picket gate that separated the yard from the barn area. Curtis kept his vehicles in the parking area next to the farm office instead of next to the house. He gave Henri and Maria the privilege of parking next to the house since he was only there on weekends. Curtis climbed into the metallic gray Ford F250 pickup and headed out the driveway.

It was only a mile over to the Mitchell's house from the Seven C Cattle Co. Roy turned into the drive at seven fifteen, not too late, just late enough to stay in Sara's good graces. He wondered why he worried so much about what Sara thought, but that answer came quickly; Sara was one of his closest friends. Dave and Sara Mitchell had stayed by his side for three straight days following that night and he was indebted to them for that. Parking his pickup with the rest of the vehicles, Roy walked around the back of the big farmhouse to the patio area.

The party was in full swing as Curtis walked through the patio gate. Sara Mitchell greeted Roy with a hug and a kiss on the cheek. Roy blushed from the attention. Sara was a petite lady with raven hair, and it always embarrassed him when his best friend's wife paid so much attention to him. Taking Roy's arm, Sara led him across the patio to a group of people hovering around the grill.

"Look who finally showed up," Sara announced to the group. "Looks like you lose the bet tonight, Dave."

"What bet?" Roy inquired. No one answered and Dave's eyes looked down at the deck. "Well, Dave, what bet?"

"Well, it's like this," Dave stammered.

"You're stalling, Dave, now out with it," Roy demanded.

"OK, I bet Steve that you wouldn't show up."

"Steve, that was like taking candy from a baby," Roy laughed. "Of course I was going to come. If I didn't Maria and Sara would have made my life unbearable."

Everyone burst out laughing at that comment and the awkwardness of the moment was gone. Sara handed Roy a large mug of sweetened iced tea and then left to mingle with the rest of the guests. Dave handed Steve the tongs so that he could watch the steaks while Dave and Roy talked. Roy and Dave sat down on a pair of wrought iron chairs. Looking at the two friends, they could have passed as brothers; both stood just over six feet tall, with broad shoulders and brown hair. Probably the only thing that was different was the goatee that Roy wore.

"I am glad that you were able to come," Dave started. "As soon as I heard that you were home from the big city, I had Sara call Maria. It's good to see you again."

"Yeah, I know. I can't believe that it has been a month since I last had a chance to get out of that rat race."

Besides owning the Seven C Cattle Co., Roy Curtis was a partner in the investment-banking firm of Lescowitch, Meier, Curtis, and Sheridan. Also one weekend a month, Roy R. Curtis, farmer and investment banker, became Lt. Col. Roy R. Curtis, United States Marine Corps Reserve, Logistics Officer for the local reserve unit in Chicago. Lescowitch, Meier, Curtis, and Sheridan was very successful and it demanded a lot of Curtis' time. The firm dealt mostly with companies that specialized in agri-business fields and Roy's farming background had proved invaluable on more than one occasion.

"So, what has been keeping you in the city instead of back here on the farm where you belong?"

"Same old stuff—mergers and acquisitions. Did you hear about the buy out of the Twin Rivers Packing Co.? That was some of my work."

"I read about it. I honestly think that it will do the producers in the area good to have a packing plant under local ownership," Mitchell commented.

"Yeah, it won't hurt," Roy replied, "and it makes a lot of business sense too. Besides, the old owners needed brought down a notch or two; I just assisted in the process. Every once in a while you have to play the pirate and do a little raiding. I notice the corn looked pretty nice coming in, how are your crops doing?"

"They are looking pretty good. We finished the new irrigation system on the back section, and it seems to be bringing the corn along really well," Dave answered. The conversation drifted on that way for the next fifteen minutes or so. First one topic then another, never too long or too serious, just two close friends catching up on each other's lives.

"I hate to break up this little reunion," Sara interrupted, "but the steaks are ready and the rest of your guests are hungry." Sara took Dave's drink and set it on the table. Taking both of his hands in hers she pulled him from his chair. Dave grabbed Sara as he rose from the chair and gave her a hug and a kiss before heading over to the main serving tables where the guests had gathered. The warming grate of the large grill was piled high with steaks as the two arrived. Taking the tongs from Steve, Dave ceremoniously presented the first steak to Roy and officially declared this party open.

Roy just shook his head and moved on down the buffet line and filled his plate. Finding a seat at a picnic table, Curtis sat down and began to eat. He looked around at all the other people laughing and having a great time and he felt suddenly lonely. *How can I feel lonely in the middle of a crowd*, he thought. It wasn't an uncommon feeling for him and it had been showing itself a lot more frequently as of late. That emptiness had first reared its ugly head shortly after his wife, Jacki, and his only son's, Brent, funeral ten years ago. It was hard to believe that ten years had passed and that Brent would have been seventeen this summer. Shaking his head in disgust, he turned back to his steak and stabbed it with his fork.

The steak was first-rate and cooked just the way he liked it, rare, or as he liked to say, skin it, dehorn it, run it by the fire, turn it around and chase it back by again, perfection. Roy focused on the succulent fare rather than his loneliness. It didn't last long anyway because the table was soon filled with friends and soon-to-be friends. Being a natural storyteller, Roy soon found himself telling some of his best tales and jokes. By the time the homemade ice cream was served, a crowd had formed including several great looking young women. Even though he was unattached, he hadn't dated anyone seriously for the last few years, and being fairly wealthy made him a good catch for any female in the area. Tonight was no exception. A brunette had settled on his right and a blonde on his left. Each was vying for his attention, but neither was getting it. With the exception of an occasional date with Carol McDaniels, a member of his recreation league volleyball team, Roy had dropped out of the dating game several years back and wasn't starting it again.

"Hi, my name's Melissa," the brunette said. She reached for the salt and let her long, tanned arm rub against his. "I am kinda new here, are you good friends of the Mitchell's?" It was not that he didn't like women, to the absolute contrary, he loved to gaze at a good-looking woman any day. Roy Curtis was just not going to play stud-in-waiting, period. Especially to a pair women with things on their minds that had nothing to do with cattle or banking.

"That's nice," Curtis said sliding a little to his left and almost into the lap of the blonde who was moving right. *I had better end this quick,* Roy thought to himself. Turning to the blonde he asked her name.

"Why it's Heather," she said with a high pitched sing-song voice that caused Roy to roll his eyes. Then with the skill and grace of an ancient swordsman he dodged and parried the women's advances. Finally Roy found an opening and disengaged himself from the two ladies. So practiced was he at drifting away that the ladies didn't realize that he was gone for at least five minutes. He looked around until he found Sara on the far side of the patio with several others, including Justin and his wife, Lisa.

He gently placed his hand on Sara's shoulder, as she turned and looked at him she knew exactly what he was going to say. She simply gave him a big hug and said good night. Sara wished that he would find someone to help him get over Jacki, but it would have to be someone extra special to fill the void left by her death.

The house was dark when Roy pulled into the driveway; Maria and Henri had gone home. The farm help was either over at Dave and Sara's or they were in Wawasee having fun. It was just as well, Roy was not in the mood to be sociable and to answer a lot of polite questions. Without turning on any of the lights, he headed to the master bedroom. In the corner of the room was a small oak stand. Curtis opened the stand and took out a square bottle. He didn't drink whiskey as a rule, but rules were meant to be broken and tonight was one of those nights. Settling in the Queen Anne recliner, Roy poured about three fingers worth into a short tumbler. He tossed it down with one swallow. It burned deep into his stomach, but not nearly as hot as the pain that was in his heart.

Looking at the bottle of sour mash, he was glad that there wasn't much left; it would not hurt as bad in the morning. There was just enough Jack Daniel's left to stupefy him tonight though, and that was what he was going to do. Drink until the pain was gone in his heart. Some shots he gulped and others he just sipped. After about an hour the empty bottle slipped through his fingers onto the floor as he lay asleep in the chair.

The alcohol did not deaden the memories or the dreams that came to haunt him. The face of his first love, Jacki, as she walked down the aisle of the church all in white, next the doctor handing him a little baby boy. Then Jacki kissing him good bye as he went off to fight in the war and the young boy holding her hand when he came home. There was a knock on the door in his dream; he knew who was behind it and didn't want to answer it, but something dragged him to it and forced him to open it. There was the patrolman with the bad news, his wife and son were dead. They had been killed in a wreck on the icy roads; a freak accident that left him with no one to blame. Flash to the cemetery as both coffins were covered and he was alone.

Over and over the dream played itself out, never changing and never ending. All night Roy tossed in the chair as he watched his wife and son being covered with dirt. He was still in the recliner when Maria came in the house early the next morning. She knocked lightly on the bedroom door and when she heard no answer she went back to the kitchen to start breakfast. The aroma of the bacon and eggs penetrated the stupor and roused Curtis from his sleep. Roy stumbled to the bathroom, each step felt as if he was caught between two sledge hammers and the goal was see if they could meet inside his head. Rubbing his hair, he gazed at himself in the mirror above the sink. His eyes were bloodshot and his clothes looked like he had worn them for a week. Slowly, trying to minimize the pain, Roy opened the medicine cabinet and took out a large bottle of Advil. Shaking four of the painkillers into his hand, he ran the water and filled the tumbler with about three fingers of water and tossed the pills and water down his throat. He wished all the Jack he consumed last night had been water. Quietly, he undressed, showered and dressed in fresh clothes. The shower had helped, but his head ached and throbbed with each movement of his body. Maybe there had been more booze in the bottle last night than he thought. With a hangover, he gingerly walked down the stairs, into the kitchen and sat down.

"Senor Curtis, drink too much last night," the housekeeper chided him. Whenever she wanted to scold Curtis, she would switch to a Spanish/English mix, though he had never spoken Spanish, the point always got across to Roy.

"I know, I know. You don't need to remind me," Curtis replied holding his head between hands. He reminded himself that consuming large quantities of alcohol was not good for oneself.

"Here, drink this. It will help ease the pain," Maria told him as she handed him a cup of tea, "at least the pain from the booze." Maria, like most of those close to Roy, knew of the demons that haunted him at night. Just like the rest of his friends, the housekeeper wished that Curtis would find someone who could chase the demons away.

"Thanks, Maria. This will help a little anyway." Roy sipped the tea. It was just the way he liked it, lukewarm almost tepid, super sweet with honey. He knew the honey would mask the taste of the shot of gin that Maria put in the tea. Roy had never liked his drinks hot and if he had his choice, as he did any morning that he was sober, he would have had a tankard of iced tea, straight up, no sugar. When he was hung over, Maria always gave him English Breakfast tea with lots of honey and a shot of alcohol. He managed to keep down an egg and bacon sandwich with lots of mustard. Maria just shook her head at his eating habits. If he didn't kill himself in his fast car, the amount of grease he consumed surely would.

"Thank you so much for breakfast," Curtis thanked Maria as he rose from the breakfast table. Roy was truly thankful for the lady who had served as nanny and housekeeper for the last four decades. "I won't be here for lunch today, but I will be here for supper. Don't give me that mother hen look. I am going riding, and right now I don't feel much like eating again."

"OK, but if you get sick and faint, and Star drags you home don't you blame me," Mrs. Gonzalez warned as she turned her back on him in fake disgust and started washing dishes.

"I love you too," Roy snapped back in the same fake anger and he headed back to his room to change. The tea, honey and the gin were all starting to work and the world was slowly stopping its spinning. Back in his room, Roy pulled on his jeans and a heavy brush popper shirt. The old bull hide boots groaned as he pulled them on. Grabbing his work Stetson and a pair of leather gloves he headed for the barn. The horses were kept in the stable and paddock next to the old bank barn where he had been unloading hay in the day before. The smell of the hay curing in the barn further served to clear the dregs of the hangover from his thick skull.

Roy stopped just inside the door and let his eyes adjust to the change in the light. There was no sense in proving Maria right by getting hurt within five minutes of leaving the house. On the wall next to the tack room hung several lead ropes. Roy took one off the nail and headed down the aisle between the stalls. As he strolled down the aisle, the horses began to stick their heads over the stall doors and whinnied as if to say, "Hello and pick me please." Curtis stopped and petted the forehead of each one as he passed by. The Seven C kept several horses each for a specific purpose. There were cutting horses like Mr. Pay and TomCat, that were used to work cattle. A couple like Danny Boy and Sara's Delight were Standard Breds and used to pull the fine carriages in parades. Curtis stopped at two of his favorites, Hezekiah and Ezekiel, two of his eight big, black Percherons that he kept to pull a big band wagon at the state fairs and large parades. Finally he arrived at his horse, Star. Star was a golden Palomino stallion with a large white spot in the middle of his forehead. People said he kept Star around because he looked liked Roy Roger's horse Trigger and that he was named after the King of the Cowboys. They were right on both accounts.

Star met Roy at the door and neighed at him. Curtis clipped the lead rope on his halter and opened the door. Star followed obediently behind Roy as he walked to the front of the barn. It was hard to believe that this same horse would love nothing better than to throw you off and run back to the barn. Roy knew what the Quarter Horse stud was capable of, because he had walked back to the barn after getting thrown on at least two occasions; once by accident and once out of pure orneriness. Even though Star seemed docile, Roy kept a firm grip on the lead rope.

Roy tossed the wool saddle blanket on him and then the old riding saddle. Curtis cinched up the straps and replaced the halter with the headstall and bit. After checking the stirrups, he led the big stallion out of the barn. Roy grabbed a lariat as he left the barn, just in case the need should arise. He grabbed the saddle horn, placed his foot in the stirrup, and stepped aboard the Palomino. Once he was firmly seated, Roy put Star through a series of starts and stops and spins just so that the horse would remember who was supposed to be in charge. Satisfied that both rider and horse were ready for the ride, Curtis pointed Star towards the pasture gate and sank his spurs into the horse's flanks. They both shot forward like a rocket and Star cleared the metal gate by at least ten inches. Leaning forward as the pair landed, Roy gave the stallion his head and let him run for five minutes before slowly pulling him down to an easy canter.

If there was a finer horse to sit upon and ride all day, Roy wasn't aware of it. The Palomino had a long, smooth gait and the rise and fall of his body was more like the waves of a gentle surf than that of a bouncing horse. President Reagan had said that there was nothing wrong with the inside of a man that the outside of a horse wouldn't cure. Curtis couldn't agree more, whenever he was lonely he went riding. Somehow setting on that stallion watching the cattle graze just seem to ease the hurt. Lately the need to ride was greater and came more often. For the next three hours he rode over the three hundred acres of the pasture and woods that contained the cattle of the Seven C Cattle Co. He looked over the herds of white faced cattle and inspected the Spring calves that would be weaned from their mothers in the next month. Roy wished that he still had someone that he could share the dreams of the farm with.

The mid-afternoon sun was beating down on him when he re-entered the paddock area. The ghosts of last night's dreams had retreated temporarily into the shadows and the hurt was deadened by the hours in the saddle. Curtis carefully removed the saddle and brushed down his horse. He grabbed a scoop of grain and put the stallion away. As he left he stopped and rubbed the nose of each horse whose big head looked over his stable door.

The aroma of food cooking met Curtis as he stepped up on the back porch. *Thank you, Maria,* Curtis thought as he entered the screen door. Even though she wasn't required to fix Sunday meals, she had put a roast and potatoes in the crock pot before she left for the day. Roy filled a large dinner plate, then he poured himself a large mug of iced tea and headed for the living room. Sunday evening would be spent doing the manly thing of eating and watching football from his recliner. It didn't take long for Curtis to empty the plate of beef and potatoes, he debated with himself whether to have seconds, but talked himself out of it. Flipping back the recliner he took a drink of tea and watched the ballgame. Tomorrow would be a better day.

Monday morning found the alarm clock clattering at four thirty. Roy was up, dressed and on the road by five fifteen. By leaving an hour earlier than he needed to, Roy could save almost two hours travel time. If he arrived in Chicago any later he would do the stop-

and-go all the way downtown. Traffic was still fairly light when he pulled into the parking garage on Van Buren St. He pulled the bright blue BMW Z4 into his reserved spot and headed to the office via the skywalks.

The firm of Lescowitch, Meier, Curtis and Sheridan Investment Bankers was founded by Paul Lescowitch's father, Adam, in the late fifties after he was discharged from the Army at the end of the Korean Conflict. The Lescowitch men had all historically been lawyers so when Adam decided to take his share of the family fortune and start an investment banking firm his family was skeptical to say the least. The family rebel, as the lawyers in the family referred to Paul's father, knew his stuff and with the help of a couple of long shot investments that paid off handsomely, he became a very rich and successful banker. One by one the firm added partners, each with their own area of expertise. The fearsome foursome, as they tended to call themselves after a couple of drinks, was completed when Mike Sheridan was offered a partnership five years earlier.

The smell of coffee brewing permeated the air as Roy walked into the office. The office administrator, Helen Peterson, usually arrived before everyone else and had the coffee ready by the time Curtis strolled in. Grabbing his cup from the stack of cups sitting by the maker, Roy poured himself a cup, added a generous amount of sugar and cream, so that it was tolerable and headed to his office. Even though he was deep in thought about the work day ahead, he managed a smile for her.

"Good morning, Mr. Curtis," Mrs. Peterson said, returning his smile with one of her own. "Just a reminder that the Copleys & Coburns will be here at nine. I have their file pulled and have you scheduled in the small conference room."

"Thank you, Mrs. Peterson, you are as efficient as always," Roy replied. Mrs. Peterson had been with the firm for almost fifteen years and knew the ins and outs of the business almost as well as the four partners did. Running the office like a military chief of staff, no one got by her unless she allowed them to. Many pushy salesman had found out the hard way that what the "slender elderly lady" at the front desk said carried as much weight as what the partners of the Lescowitch, Meier, Curtis & Sheridan said. Roy and Mike Sheridan had laughed more than once as the lovely Mrs. Peterson escorted a salesman from the office after he had tried to bypass her.

Roy settled in behind his desk and started reading the file on the Copleys & Coburns Trading Company LLC. They were looking to expand into the Asian market and were hoping to arrange financing through LMC&S. Curtis knew it would be a long day and just hoped he could survive some of the pettiness of the banking world. The day rolled on with phone calls, e-mails and faxes demanding his attention. Some of them wanting to buy, some to sell, but all wanting money one way or the other. For Roy, it was just another typical day at the office; the kind that sustains life but gives nothing to live for.

# Chapter 2

She had just finished giving the oil filter a final twist to snug it into place when the phone rang. Reluctantly, Becca pushed the creeper out from under the school bus and headed towards the phone.

"I am never going to get these buses serviced before the evening route at this rate," she muttered to herself. Rebecca Davidson was the bus superintendent and head mechanic, which also meant the only mechanic, for the small school district. She had been at this job for fifteen years, taking it after her husband had left her and a small daughter for some tramp two counties over.

Becca had met Frank Davidson at the race track when she was fresh out of high school. He had raised himself out from under the hood of the stock car he had been working on and looked straight into her heart. Frank Davidson had wasted no time wondering about this knockout of a young girl and had promptly asked her out. Becca had only hesitated long enough to swallow the lump that had formed in her throat before saying yes. That evening had been wonderful, Becca sat there cow-eyed as Frank had gone on and on about stock cars and motors and drivers. Nobody had ever paid that kind of attention to her before and she was mesmerized. Even though she was five years his junior, she had thought nothing of it. She thought it was love and would have followed him anywhere. In fact, Becca had followed him everywhere. To every race track in a two hundred mile radius, she followed him.

It was after a race upstate in a little diner as they drank bad coffee and ate grilled cheese sandwiches that Frank had proposed and she had agreed to marry him. For the next three years, Becca's life was idyllic as far as she was concerned. Frank's race team was winning, they were traveling together more and more. Races on the weekends, go home and spend the first part of the week in the apartment snuggling and enjoying each other. During that time she had watched Frank and the other mechanics as they tuned the engines to get every ounce of horsepower that was available from the engines. Becca learned about suspensions and tires and fuel consumption. She waited patiently at the edge of the pits and watched, and then over a beer or coffee, she would ask questions. Not the kind of questions that sounded like she was prying, but the kind of questions that made the guys want to talk and impress the crew chief's woman.

They had been married for just over three years when Becca had proudly announced that she was pregnant. Frank had given her a polite hug and then had promptly gone back to work under the car. The farther along Becca progressed with the pregnancy, the more distant Frank became. About a month before she was due to deliver, he had informed her that she was no longer allowed in the pit area. On a cold damp Tuesday in April, Becca gave birth to a six pound eight ounce bundle of joy named Rachael, while Frank was racing dirt track in Missouri.

After Rachael's birth, Becca had tried to rejoin the boys in the pits, but the demands of motherhood kept her at home. Frank was home even less than before, electing often to stay with the crew rather than drive the hour home. To pass the time, Becca had wandered over to her grandparent's house. When Grandpa Reid asked her to drive the tractor and baler during hay season she gladly agreed. Becca spent her summers driving the tractor with Rachael strapped in a car seat that was welded to the fender of the John Deere

4020. Winter rolled around and Becca found herself helping repair the machinery. She learned quickly from her grandpa the intricacies of the diesel engine. Applying what she had learned in the race pits and from Grandpa Reid, she soon had more than enough work to keep her busy fixing tractors and farm equipment.

Rachael was just four years old when it occurred. It was early spring and Frank was racing in Plattsburg and should have been home that night. Becca had waited and worried as the evening hours ticked by. Finally at three in the morning she had fallen asleep on the sofa. The next morning when she awakened, she started to call the police when the telephone rang. It was Frank.

The conversation was short and sweet. *That's not correct,* Becca thought later, *conversation requires two people to exchange words and this had been all one-sided.* An edict was a more appropriate word. Frank had spoken them and hung up.

"I don't love you anymore and I have found someone else," he said in a rehearsed tone, "the boys will be over to pick up my stuff." With that he hung up. Those were the last words that Becca ever heard him say. Throughout the divorce, which she did not protest, they only spoke through their attorneys. So with a small monthly amount for child support, Becca had been thrust on her own. She had cried a lot, asked why a lot, screamed a lot. In the end, she had put on her coveralls and headed to the shop.

She spent long hours in the shop fixing equipment, often until the wee hours in the morning. Rebecca managed to make enough money so that she and Rachael stayed in the apartment that they had been living in before Frank had left. Becca longed for a steady job with fixed hours. She laughed at the thought of being a waitress or a secretary, so when the school district had advertised for a mechanic she had applied and surprised even herself when she got the position.

The job had been rough at first, but she managed to turn the small, run-down fleet of buses into one of the best in the state. More than once she had quietly thanked her grandfather for teaching her about diesel engines. Year after year the fleet had passed the state inspections with no problems.

"Hello, bus garage, Ms. Davidson speaking." Rebecca spoke as authoritatively as possible. She had come to expect all kinds of patronizing from salesmen to teachers when they called. The idea of a good-looking woman being a mechanic somehow didn't quite fit with the stereotypes that they had in their heads and Becca definitely fell into the category of good-looking women. Some of her suitors would have said great-looking. At five foot nine inches, she looked fantastic in jeans or a dress. Her blue eyes and flame-red hair served as proof of her Celtic blood, while her high cheek bones and smooth skin showed traces of a Native American heritage. Propping the phone to her ear with her shoulder, Becca took the rag from her coveralls pocket and wiped her hands.

"Becca, this is Linda in the office." Linda Swartz was the school secretary and one of the few people who were actually glad that a woman ran the bus garage. "There is a Mr. Benson here to see you. He says he is from a university and Becca, he is good looking."

Becca chuckled. Linda Swartz had been trying to set her up with a man for the last ten years and Becca had to admit that she had been on a couple of great dates because of it. "Linda, if he is breathing, then he is a good-looking man to you. Send him on back."

"I don't think he is dressed to go back to the shop area, you had better come up here."

"OK, give me five minutes to put oil back in bus 3 and wash up."

"I will tell him. Bye."

"Bye."

Quickly she poured the quarts of oil into the bus engine. Her mind raced from one idea to another as she tried to place this Mr. Benson and why he wanted to see her. Maybe he wanted to do some kind of research on bus safety. Becca had been published in a couple of trade magazines on bus safety. That was it, that was the only reason that made sense. She tightened the fill cap and shut the hood on the bus. Rebecca took off her coveralls and hung them on the hook by the lockers. As Becca washed up, she was glad that she had chosen to wear a decent shirt and pair of jeans instead of the skimpy tank top and cut offs she normally wore. Both barely covered the essential areas of her body, but they were comfortable to wear under the work clothes. A quick run of the brush through her hair and she was out the door.

Becca entered the back way to the school office and Linda pointed at the gentleman sitting in the waiting area. Taking a deep breath to calm her, Becca walked over to him. The gentleman put down the paper he was reading and stood up as she approached. Linda had been right; he was fairly good looking, not a movie star by any means, but handsome. He flashed a large smile and extended his hand. Becca noticed the wedding ring and immediately wiped any romantic notions form her mind.

"Ms. Davidson? I am Ralph Benson, with Moluntha State University over in the Quad Cities."

"Glad to meet you, please call me Becca." Becca took his hand and shook it. *Good*, she thought, *a good strong handshake, not a wimp by any means.* "What can I do for you today, Mr. Benson?"

"Do we have someplace we can talk, Ms. Davidson? I mean Becca."

"Sure the faculty lounge is this way," she said, pointing down the hall. "It shouldn't be too busy this time of day."

"Excellent. Lead the way."

Becca led the way to the teacher's lounge. Getting a cup of coffee for both of them, Becca sat down at a round table in the corner.

"Ms. Davidson, I don't know how to put this exactly." Mr. Benson looked down at his coffee. "I mean I was expecting a teacher, not a bus driver, when I came here."

The redheaded temper of Becca Davidson flared to the same shade as her hair. It took full restraint not to throw the cup of hot coffee in his lap and storm out of the room. The chauvinistic snob how dare he think such thoughts. She started to rise to leave.

"Please, let me explain," he said, motioning her to sit and pulling a copy of a magazine out of his briefcase at the same time. "The university received a copy of your article that you had written for *The Western Cowboy* magazine and the faculty of the western cultures was extremely impressed. The bio said that you worked for the school and the university sent me to contact you. I assumed, obviously wrongly assumed, that you were a teacher here."

Becca's temper subsided a little at the apology. "You said contact. Why may I ask? Did I offend somebody?"

"Oh, no, quite the opposite. The university would like you to expand your article and present it at the fall Native American conference next month. I know it is short notice, so the university only expects a half hour or so lecture," Mr. Benson said.

"What can I say but wow? I am honored, a little overwhelmed, but honored to say the least. I would be glad to present my paper at the conference."

"Good," Benson said. "Out of personal curiosity, how did you become interested in the Sioux Tribe and end up writing that article?"

"I guess I always have been interested in Indians," she told him. "I know that is not the politically correct term for them, but that is how I think of them. Growing up, my family lived in the middle of Nebraska, the middle of nowhere too most people, but I loved the area. I would walk the freshly plowed ground with my younger cousin and look for arrowheads and artifacts. We accumulated buckets full of them. Some of it was junk, but most were very good, and as I know now, very rare artifacts. One day as I was talking to my grandmother she told me that one of my ancestors was the daughter of a Sioux chief and then I was really hooked. I spent every spare moment during high school learning about the Sioux nation, specifically the Lakota's. I am always buying magazines and books about the old west and subscribe to *The Western Cowboy*. About two years ago, I got this wild idea to submit an article on the Lakota Sioux and the result is what you have in your hand. It has been a cross between a hobby and a border-line obsession for me all my life."

"I am glad you accepted, Ms. Davidson, I mean Becca." Mr. Benson extended his hand. "I think you will be the breath of fresh air that the conference needs. I will clear it with the committee and have a contract drawn up. The university will be in touch with more details. If I can get a telephone number and mailing address, I think we will be concluded for today. I know how busy you must be."

"Thank you so much." Becca gave him her cell phone number and personal post office box. Living alone for all these years she had gotten out of the habit of giving her home address to anyone and she wasn't about to start now. She walked him back to the office where he signed out.

"It has truly been a pleasure meeting you. Have a good day," Mr. Benson said as he turned and exited the office. As he crossed the parking his heart pounded and a fine layer of sweat broke out on his forehead.

"Ralph, you really did it this time," he muttered to himself. For the last five years he had been trying to persuade the planning committee to invite non-PhD's to be conference speakers. He had finally found one whose writing impressed the committee enough to convince them that he was correct. They had sent him out to invite her personally, and she turns out to be a mechanic.

As he buckled himself in his car and headed back towards the Quad Cities, his mind raced and his stomach flipped. About half way back down the freeway, a plan formulated in his brain. It would take a little arm twisting and chip playing. If he pulled it off, it would save his face and allow his new-found speaker to be the first non-professor ever to speak at the Native American Conference.

"So what was that all about?" Linda asked as soon as the door shut behind Mr. Benson.

"The university wants me to speak at their fall conference," Davidson replied.

"On what? How come? How'd they find you?" Swartz questioned her in rapid-fire sequence.

"One question at a time. First of all, they would like me to speak on the Lakota Sioux Tribal life. How come? Because they liked my article that was published in *The Western Cowboy*, that's why. He thought I was a teacher here at the school."

"That's why he looked so at you so strangely when you walked in here dressed like that."

"Yeah, can you imagine how he'd looked at me if I would have been wearing a tank top or my bathing suit like I do in the summer?" Becca and Linda both chuckled at that thought.

"I didn't know you wrote," Linda commented. "Have you published anything else?"

"It's a hobby of mine, something to do instead of staying home and watching the tube. I have sent articles to several magazines, but only two have been published. The first was a short article of the Little Big Horn River basin that *Wyoming Life* magazine ran about two years ago and then this one in *The Western Cowboy* on tribal life of the Lakota Sioux. Not real interesting stuff, but I like it," Becca shrugged her shoulders. "Besides I made enough to pay for a new satellite dish."

Linda shook her head and chuckled, "You are a paradox, Becca Davidson, a paradox."

"Well, the oil still needs changed in the last two buses so I had better get back to the garage. Do you really think he will contact me, Linda?"

"He sounded serious to me, even if you are only a bus mechanic."

"Oh, shut up!" With that Becca headed out the door back to the bus garage. *Wow*, she thought as she walked, *if this isn't a dream come true. Now if I could only meet someone tall, dark and handsome, I would be set for life.*

The rest of the day was a blur; somehow she managed to get the oil changed in the rest of the busses. All that she could think about was the amount of research she needed to do to turn her article into an interesting half hour lecture. That was the key to writing and lecturing, wasn't it? If you had all your facts together, but still put the crowd to sleep, you hadn't accomplished anything.

On the way home, she stopped at the supermarket to pick up some things for supper. Rachael was coming over and she could hardly wait to tell her. She thought about calling her then, but decided to break the news to her over supper. With an exhilarated step she went down the aisles of the store, picking up the ingredients needed for a Mexican stew complete with cayenne and red-chili peppers. Quickly she paid for the items and headed back to her dark green Jeep Cherokee.

The message light was flashing on her cell phone when she climbed into the front seat. Without thinking, Becca flipped the button to retrieve the message. Plugging the speaker into the phone, she backed out and started out of the parking lot.

"Hello, Ms. Davidson. This is Ralph Benson," the first message started. Becca prepared herself for the rejection then and there. That was the only reason he would call so quickly. "I want to apologize for not giving you more details this afternoon, but I had to report to the university first. I have been given the OK, so here are the specifics. The conference will take place October twenty-third and twenty-fourth; your lecture will be forty-five minutes in length. We will need your abstract and outline no later than the fifth of the month. I am sending you a contract in the mail tomorrow, please look it over and if you have any questions call me at 555-8674. Thank you."

Becca just about wrecked the Jeep. They really wanted for her ability and not because she was a teacher. She punched on the radio and turned it up. Her hands danced across the steering wheel as she listened to country music. She was sure that the neighbors would be giving her dirty looks for playing her music so loud, frankly she didn't care. She was in a great mood and nothing was going to spoil it.

Becca lived in a small subdivision on the east side of town. It had been the developer's idea to bring a little of the city to the small town, so it was a mix of brick townhouses and single family homes with plenty of common green spaces for relaxing in. Becca had bought her townhouse about nine years before. The two-story dwelling had fitted her and her daughter's needs perfectly. The garage was attached in the rear of the house with a large deck next to it. Pulling into her garage, she shut the Jeep off and carried the bags of food inside. Supper was going to be a celebration. Pots and pans were pulled from the cupboard; spices and herbs were added to the vegetables and meat she had purchased from the store.

"Hi, Mom, it's me!" Rachael hollered as she entered the front door. The stew had been cooking for about a half an hour when Rachael arrived and the kitchen was filled with its spicy aroma. Rachael Davidson was nineteen and shared an apartment with two other girls in Eagleton, where she worked as a graphics designer. She was the spitting image of her mother when Becca was her age, except for the blonde hair, and she was not quite as tall.

"Smells good," Rachael said. "When do we eat?" Rachael gave her mom a big hug and looked into the pot. The steam and fragrance rose as Rachael lifted the lid. After taking a big whiff, she replaced the lid and opened the cupboard where the dishes were kept. As she placed the dishes on the table, she couldn't help but notice the exuberance of her mother as Becca busied herself in the kitchen. Rachael took her place at the table as Becca dished up the stew. Dying of curiosity, she asked, as soon as her mom sat down at the table.

"OK, Mom, what's up?" Rachael asked. "You have that 'I just stole the cookies' look all over you."

"You are not going to believe it, Rach, but I got a visit today from Moluntha State University."

"And?"

"They want me to present a lecture at their fall conference on Native American Culture."

"No, you're kidding."

"Seriously. They read my article in *The Western Cowboy* and what want me to expand on it."

"Boy, they must be desperate."

"Very funny, Rach. Ha-ha."

"Really, Mom, I think it is super cool," she said, giving her mother a high five. "Are you going to have time to get it ready?"

"Yeah, I should be able to, the basic research is all done so it is just a matter of putting it into lecture format. It will be work but I can do it."

"Mom, do they know you are a bus mechanic and not a teacher?"

"Oh yeah, you should have seen Mr. Benson's expression, he's the man from the university, when I walked into the office wiping my hands with a grease rag. He caught on quickly that I am not your average mechanic."

"No kidding. How many other mechanics do you know that wear Frederick's of Hollywood under their coveralls? You *were* dressed properly, weren't you?"

With that Becca leaned back and laughed. Rach had the timing of a professional comedian and could always make her laugh. "Yes, dear, jeans and a shirt today. Too cold for the halter top and Daisy Mae shorts." The rest of the meal was spent exchanging small talk about work and life in general. During dessert the conversation took the normal turn towards guys and love. It always happened whenever the two of them got together; the only question was who would bring it up first. Becca and Rach were open with each other about their personal lives, and had worked through a lot of difficult times as Rachael grew up. Rachael was dishing up the ice cream when Becca switched the talk over to guys.

"So, Rach, how is the guy situation over in Eagleton?"

"Not real good right at the moment, Mom. I went out with a guy a couple of times, but he seemed more interested in getting me in the sack than getting to know me. We would go out to eat and his hands would be all over me. One of those international guys."

"You mean Roman Hands and Russian Fingers?"

"Yep, and it didn't matter where we were either. Maybe if he would have had a little more tact as to when, it might have been fun, but it was so bad I couldn't handle it. How about you? Any new loves in my bodacious mother's life?"

"No, just the same old jerks who hang out at the race track. Oh, there are a couple of guys that look nice, but most of them think that there is no way a girl can know the difference between a distributor cap and an overhead cam. Tom Nelsh has asked me out a couple of time, but I have turned him down."

"Why? He's cute, nice bod."

"That's the main problem—he is good looking and he knows it. Just ask him, he'll tell you. He lacks a little upstairs, too," Becca answered. The rest of the dessert went that way, mother and daughter comparing their non-existent love and social lives. After they had finished, they both grabbed a cup of coffee and retired to the living room for a movie. The movie was one of Becca's favorites but she didn't watch it. Tonight for some reason she felt lonelier than usual, even with Rachael sitting in the other chair. It was that nagging void that was in her life, the void that was caused by the absence of a man to snuggle up against. She had felt it before and would feel it again. As long as she lived alone, the emptiness would be there.

When the movie was over, Rach gave her mother a hug and headed back to Eagleton. Becca knew she needed to go to bed, but tonight she couldn't face the bed by herself. She slipped off her jeans, curled up under a blanket and tried to sleep on the couch. For an hour she just stared at the ceiling, her mind racing about what had transpired that day. How would she ever get the presentation ready in time? Could she make it interesting enough to keep people's attention? Would they laugh at her? Would she do the history of the Sioux Tribe justice? Thoughts and questions raced through her mind one right after another, until she finally drifted off to sleep.

# Chapter 3

Regardless of how much work needed to be done, the office always shut down at four-thirty on Friday afternoon. Paul Lescowitch set that rule hard and fast in the early days of the firm. He was under the opinion that if all you did was work you would work yourself in an early grave. Paul thought that by giving the staff a chance to relax, he was saving them from that early grave. Sometimes they all gathered around the corner from the office at McMurphy's Bar & Grill, where Mike and Roy would entertain everyone with karaoke. That was not the case tonight. After a week of wheeling and dealing, Roy was ready to head to the farm. His workload was enough to keep him busy all weekend, but the cowboy in him called and he needed to go riding.

So at four thirty-seven, the blue Z4 headed out of Chicago toward the big northern Indiana farm. Though he spent his week in the city, Roy was in constant contact with Justin. More than once he thanked the gentleman that created the cell phone and nationwide long distance calling. Justin was liable to call from the cab of a tractor or the back of a horse. Roy answered the cell phone on the second ring.

"Hey, Justin, how's it going?" Curtis inquired.

"Pretty good. Are you coming to the farm this weekend?" Roberts replied.

"Yeah, I am on my way right now, should be there about eight. What's up?"

"Nothing is wrong. I just figured if you were coming out and weren't busy we could wean and sort calves tomorrow."

"Sounds good to me," Roy answered. It would be hard work but the kind of work Roy loved to do. "Were you thinking of sleeping in late or starting at first light?"

"First light if you don't stay out and party all night long," Justin joked. "Honestly, if we could get started at seven we could get most of the sorting done by noon."

"Seven with spurs on. Bye." With that, Roy flipped the phone shut leaving Roberts talking to thin air. At the farm, Justin just shook his head and pocketed the phone.

The dust off the gravel drive plumed into the air as the BMW pulled into its parking spot next to Roy's pickup. The light was still on in the kitchen and Curtis wondered what Maria was doing at the house so late. The question was answered as soon as Roy opened the door. The aroma of freshly baked pumpkin pie enveloped him as he entered. The housekeeper was just dishing up a piece and applying a generous helping of fresh whipped cream to the top.

"Justin stopped by on his way home and said you would be here tonight," Maria said. The housekeeper set the plate down and Roy reached out to give her a hug and a peck on the cheek. At five feet two inches, the Mexican lady barely made it to Curtis' arm. She was just like family and Roy greeted her as he would any other aunt. "I thought you might want a snack while you watch the game tonight. Henri picked some pumpkins this afternoon so you get the first pie of the season."

"Thanks, Maria," Curtis said taking the pie and heading for the living room. "Oh by the way, I will be helping Justin and the crew tomorrow so you won't have to make breakfast for me. I will just grab a bite of something on the way out to the barn."

"OK. I will see you when I bring lunch out to the crew," Maria replied.

Roy sat in the recliner, switched on the TV, and looked for a game. The advantage of satellite TV was you could always find a game to watch. After surfing through a half a dozen channels, he settled on a hockey game. As he ate the fresh pie and watched the game, the stress of the week seemed to melt away. Before long Roy found himself fighting to keep his eyes open. Clicking the remote, he took his empty plate to the kitchen, put it in the sink and headed up to his bedroom.

The alarm rang early and Roy was up and going, refreshed from an unusually restful sleep. Grabbing an old pair of jeans and a work shirt, he dressed quickly. Passing through the kitchen on his way out the door, he spied the pie sitting under glass on the counter. With a smile, Curtis grabbed a piece of pie and headed out to his truck.

It was a crisp fall morning and a light fog was rising from the river as Curtis pulled into the barnyard on the back side of the farm. The lights were on in the barn and the clang of gates echoed from within. Roy parked the Ford and made his way to the barn.

Sorting cattle isn't one of the most glamorous jobs around a ranch, but probably one of the most satisfying to Roy. It was the finish to a year's worth of work. Everything that a cowman did led up to the day when the calves were weaned and sorted.

"Morning, Roy. You ready to get at it?" Justin greeted him. Justin and half a dozen cowhands were waiting at the far end of the barn. There were a string of horses tied to the fence.

"Good morning, gentlemen," Roy answered back and then walked over to the horses. Reaching up he petted the nose of a big chestnut gelding and whispered in his ear. The horse recognized him and nuzzled him back. Roy continued to stroke him and check the saddle and rigging until he was satisfied that everything was ready.

"Well, TomCat, are you ready to get some work done?" Roy grabbed the reins and stepped into the saddle. The rest of the guys grabbed their horses and followed suit. Justin led the way out of the corral area and out into the pasture. Even though the farm owned several ATVs, Roy and Justin preferred using horses when it came to sorting and working with the cattle. Justin contended and Roy agreed that the animals stayed quieter than when they were herded with the ATVs.

The Seven C Cattle Co. had about two hundred-fifty brood cows, most of which calved in the early spring. So as soon as the grass started to dry in late September-early October, the calves would be weaned and either kept as breeding stock, sold as feeders, or fed out as beef for sale. The eight cowboys spread out across the pasture and began to drive the cattle towards the barn.

TomCat was an excellent cow pony and soon Roy felt he was just along for the ride. If a calf decided to bolt for the back pasture, the big chestnut was cutting him off before Curtis had a chance to react. It took about an hour to round up the one hundred seventy-five cows and their calves and another hour to put them in the corrals. Finally around nine a.m. they started the actual sorting process. First the cows and calves were separated and the cows headed back out to pasture. Then the heifers and bulls were split into their respective corrals.

It was close to noon. Roy and Justin were leaning on the fence looking over the heifers when Maria's gray Dodge minivan pulled up to the barn. Henri and Maria got out and went to work. Soon tables had been set up and a feast was ready to be served. The crew sat down and began to eat, Maria hovering over the guys making sure that their glasses stayed full of Pepsi or iced tea. As the crew ate and talked of the morning, Roy had to wonder why he chose to do anything else.

# Chapter 4

The month flew by for Becca, between the buses, field trips, and preparing for the conference, there was not much time left. Every free moment she was on her laptop, writing and re-writing her notes. She called Ralph Benson almost daily, running ideas and thoughts by him for his opinion. He always took her calls and offered sound advice whenever possible. At one point during the month, she wondered if she and her laptop were one. If only she and her ex-husband had spent half as much time together, they might be married still. She knew that if her speech was properly prepared, she could deliver it and keep the crowd's attention.

Becca arrived at her hotel the evening before the conference was to begin. The Quad Cities were a fairly easy drive to the west from her place and she could have done it in the morning without much stress, but the university had offered her a room and she accepted graciously. If she could relax in the hot tub and have a quiet evening, and somebody else pay for it then who was she to complain. Opening her garment bag, she took out her suit that she would wear tomorrow and hung it up. Becca finished unpacking and the changed into her swimsuit. She had left the bikini at home and had opted instead to bring her one-piece suit. It was bright blue and high-cut. It showed off her long legs nicely and just enough cleavage was revealed that men would turn and look. Putting on the robe that the hotel supplied and grabbing her towel, she headed down to the pool area. The pool area was almost empty when Becca arrived. She placed her robe and towel on a lounge chair, and slipped into the hot tub to relax.

The jets of water massaged her body as she leaned back and closed her eyes. The tension of preparing the lecture slowly drained from her body. Becca's thoughts drifted from the text of tomorrow's presentation to wondering what it would have been like to live with the Sioux on the plains one hundred and fifty years ago. She relaxed in a dream-like state until the timer went off on the tub. Reluctantly, Becca climbed out of the now quiet hot tub and dove into the pool. The contrast of the heat of the hot tub and the coolness of the pool invigorated her. After a couple of hard laps, she flipped onto her back and floated for a while. Swimming to the end where her stuff was, she climbed out and walked over to the lounge chair. Toweling herself dry, she slipped her robe back on and walked over to the vending machines. Dropping in her coins, she selected a diet cola and headed back poolside.

It felt nice to recline in the chair and Becca was in no mood to return by herself to an empty room, so she sat and watched as others came and went from the pool area. Most of the time being alone did not bother her, after all a single parent's life is being alone at least half the time. Lately though, the emptiness was greater and more frequent than it had been in a long time. As Becca Davidson watched couples and families play in the water together, she had to wonder what it would be like to have a steady man in her life. Sadly she just shook her head, knowing that that possibility was very remote. Finally she told herself that she had moped long enough. She headed back to her room for a night of lonely sleep.

Becca was up early the next morning; the loneliness of the previous night was gone, replaced by the awareness of having to make her presentation. Becca was in high gear today. She had to be perfect and she was ready. Like a large cat she paced the room, going over and over her presentation. Buttoning the last button on her vest, she pulled on her jacket and looked in the mirror. *Nice, very nice*, she thought. The pinstripe suit looked professional, at the same time very feminine.

"If nothing else," she said out loud, "The men will watch me, even if I am boring." Putting on her pumps, she grabbed her laptop and case and headed out the door. Even though the room had been paid for by the university, Becca still checked out and got the receipt, just in case. The hotel dining room had a breakfast buffet, but Becca was too nervous to eat very much, so she ordered a cup of hot tea and a bagel. The last thing she needed was for her empty stomach to growl during the speech. She watched the hotel's guests file in and out of the dining area as she ate. Paying the bill and tipping the waiter, she headed out the door toward her vehicle.

It was a short trip to the university, and Mr. Benson had provided her with detailed directions. Moluntha State University was located on the eastern edge of the Quad Cities area. According to the brochure that the university had sent her in her speaker's packet, Moluntha State University was over one hundred and fifty years old. Becca turned onto the boulevard where the main entrance was located and was amazed at the beauty she saw. The buildings were close together but great care had been taken to landscape the area for beauty and quietness. The shrubs and trees were ablaze with their fall colors. Here and there, park benches had been placed in alcoves created by the landscapers. Even in the early morning hours, Becca could see couples sitting and talking on the benches.

"Are you here for the conference, ma'am?" the young college co-ed, in an orange reflective vest labeled "Traffic," asked as Becca turned into the large parking lot next to the conference center.

"Yes, I am presenting one of the sessions," Becca replied.

"Very good, if you will head down that row," the girl pointed to a row of cars two rows to her left, "at the far end is the speaker's entrance. Show the doorman your credentials, he will let you in and have a valet park your Jeep."

"Thank you very much, and have a good day."

"You have a good day also, ma'am."

Becca turned down the row that the young lady had indicated and drove to the far end. The doorman, also a college student, opened her door and took Becca's laptop case from her. Speaking into his radio, he summoned a valet to park her Cherokee.

"Ms. Davidson, you may pick up your car here when you are ready to leave. The doorman on duty will have your keys. If you will go down the hallway to your right, you will find Mr. Benson in the speaker's lounge. He will make sure that you get set up."

"Thank you and have a nice day." Becca made her way down the hall and found the lounge with ease. The lounge was set up with a few writing tables in the far corner for the speakers to work at, but the rest of the room contained sofas and several big easy chairs for the speakers to relax in. The smell of fresh-brewed coffee permeated the room. Mr. Benson was talking to one of the other speakers, when Becca walked in the room. Immediately he excused himself and walked over to greet her.

"Such a delight to see you again, Becca." Ralph Benson extended his hand in greeting. They had dropped the formality and were on a first name basis, due mostly to their daily conversations and partly because they had become genuine friends over the last month as Becca had been preparing for today. Ralph had taken her under his wing and had made sure that she had been well prepared. Not that she had needed much help, he had to admit to himself, it was that he had argued to keep her on the agenda after the committee had found out that she wasn't an educator.

"Thank you, Ralph," Becca replied. "I hope I don't look too nervous, but I am."

"You look just fine." Ralph smiled. He remembered the meeting when he had told the rest of the committee that Becca was a mechanic and how one of the professors had argued that she would come looking like one. Well, he was definitely wrong about that, Ms. Davidson looked every bit the educator today. "I have your schedule here." He consulted a folded piece of Franklin paper in his hand. "You are to speak in room 223 during the second and fourth sessions, once before lunch and right afterward. The room monitor has all your outlines and will see to the power point presentation for you, all you will have to do is speak. I know that sounds easy enough. Please have a cup of coffee and relax."

Determined to do her best to relax, Becca settled into a large easy chair, drank a cup of coffee, and reviewed her notes. About fifteen minutes before she was due to speak, one of Mr. Benson's assistants came for her. She followed him down the corridor to the room. A quick set of instructions and review of her outline by the room moderator and she was up. The butterflies hit full force as she crossed the platform to the lectern. Becca was shaking as she set her notes down. Taking a deep breath, she held on to the side of the oak lectern and began. The first words were a little shaky, but once she got going, the passion of her research came out and she presented the lecture with fervor and pride. The rest of the speech went smoothly, the slides and pictures brought the dimension that she had hoped and with just one minute to spare she finished up. Then the audience was allowed to ask questions, which they did with the vigor of a White House press conference. The best she could, Becca fielded and answered each one. When the moderator stepped on to the platform to close the session, the room gave her a hearty thank you with a generous round of applause.

Becca didn't think it could get any better, but it did. Confident from the morning session, she spoke with enthusiasm in the afternoon. That session went as smoothly as the first and Becca was a little disappointed when the last person had filed out of the room afterward. *This has been fun,* she thought, *a lot of work in preparation but fun.* She had always been a student of American History, but to have been a teacher of it was exhilarating. She was putting the last of her notes away when an elderly gentleman approached from the rear of the room. Becca remembered seeing him there during both sessions and wondered who he was.

"Very good presentation, Ms. Davidson." The gentleman extended his hand, withered slightly with age it still possessed a strong grip. "I am Dr. Houchin, Chairman of the History Department and I would like to congratulate you on a job well done."

"That is most gracious of you," Becca replied. "I was a little scared to begin with."

"I wondered if you would be able to pull it off. I want you to know that I was not in favor of you speaking, but I am glad you did. If all the professors in this department would speak with such passion, people would come to love history."

"Why thank you again, I am flattered."

"If you are not in a big hurry to leave, Ms. Davidson, I would like to talk to you in my office after the conference," Dr. Houchin requested.

"No, I am not in a hurry. In fact, now that I am done speaking, I was hoping to be able to sit in on the last couple of sessions."

"That should be no problem," Dr. Houchin assured her. "I will speak to Mr. Benson about our meeting. He will make sure you get to my office afterward." With that comment, Dr. Houchin left the auditorium.

The rest of the afternoon went quickly for Becca. She looked through the list of speakers and chose two subjects that interested her, one on Lakota tribal life and another on the history of the Shoshone tribe. Both were interesting and she could hardly believe the day was over. Quickly she worked her way back to the speaker's lounge to meet Mr. Benson.

"Becca, you must have made quite an impression on Dr. Houchin. He has summoned his staff to meet with you in his office in fifteen minutes so we need to leave right away," Ralph said. Leading the way to his car, Ralph opened the passenger door and helped her in. *How long had it been since that happened?* Becca thought and they raced across campus. The history department was located, appropriately, in the oldest building on the campus. The brick building seemed to ooze with character and history. Ralph led her to Dr. Houchin's office; the massive oak door had a brass plaque on it that read *Dwight A. Houchin Ph. D., Chairman History Department*. The door groaned as she opened it. Seated in overstuffed chairs was the staff of the history department. Dr. Houchin welcomed her and made the proper introductions. Becca only caught a couple of the names and she made a mental note to asked Benson for a list if they ever met again.

"Ms. Davidson, I am speaking for the whole department when I say that we were impressed with your lecture today." Becca started to speak but Dr. Houchin stopped her. "We would love to have you join us on the faculty, but your lack of an advanced degree precludes that from happening." Becca wondered what they were leading up to if they couldn't hire her on the faculty.

"However," Dr. Houchin continued, "the department has been talking about starting a new program for some time, but we haven't been able to find the right person. Today, we found that person in you. Let me explain what the program is about and what we would like you to do. We, and by we I mean the department, has been concerned for some time that the only image that children today have of the Native American is that of a savage, which you and I both know is wrong. What we would like to do is to send a person around to the schools to change that image. After seeing your presentation and talking with you, we all agree that you are the person for the job.

"If you take this job, and we sincerely hope that you do, we will give you an office and an assistant and handle all of the scheduling. We will try to send you out only once a week to begin with so you will be able to maintain your present job as a bus supervisor. Any questions or comments?"

"I am totally surprised and overwhelmed. Would you mind if I took the weekend to sort everything out and give you an answer, say, Monday afternoon?"

"Yes, by all means. I will expect your call Monday afternoon," Dr. Houchin replied. "If you don't have any more questions, I will wish you a good day as I am very tired from today's conference." With that, Dr. Houchin rose out of the chair and left. The other members shook Becca's hand and congratulated her as they left.

The trip home was a blur. She had thought that she was overwhelmed when they had asked her to speak at the conference, but this was overwhelming times ten. How could she teach? She was only a mechanic. The battle in her mind continued all weekend, until

Rachael came over Sunday afternoon.

"What's up, Mom? You look beat," her daughter inquired.

"Can I say I am excited to death?" Becca started. "Sit down and I will tell you about it. Do you want something to drink?"

"A cup of Earl Grey would be nice, thanks." Nothing was said while Becca heated the water in the microwave. Grabbing a tray of cookies, she brought them and two mugs to the wooden kitchen table and sat down. "OK, Mom, I am dying of curiosity, so let's have it."

"You know I spoke yesterday at Moluntha State University."

"Yeah, how did it go?" Rach interrupted.

"Fine, let me finish will you?"

"OK, OK."

"Anyway, yesterday went perfectly. I was a little nervous, but once I got started, the presentation went great. I did so well I even impressed the chairman of the department. Afterward he invited me to his office for a meeting with the entire department." Becca then related the details of the meeting with Dr. Houchin and his staff. When she was done talking, Becca looked at Rachael, who sitting with her head in her hands, staring at her mom.

"Mom, that is absolutely fantastic. Can you imagine how many people would love to be paid for their passion?"

"I know, but what about my job at the school?"

"Don't worry about it. It was only supposed to fill the gap after Dad left. You said that yourself. Now that I am out of the house, go and do what you want. If the university wants you bad enough they will pay you for your time."

"I suppose you are correct as always." Becca had to agree with her daughter. Rachael had a good head on her shoulders and usually could analyze a situation and come up with the correct answer.

"Now that's settled, let's talk about something important."

"Like what?"

"Guys," Rachael said matter of factly. With that they both laughed.

Becca was up bright and early Monday morning. She knew that she was going to have to break the news to the superintendent and she wasn't looking forward to it. She always tried to look professional when she met with any of the administration so she pulled on a blue oxford with the school logo and a pair of navy slacks with her boots. Her stomach did flips as she drove her Cherokee down the street toward the school. Becca parked up near the offices instead of around back by the bus barn.

"Hi, how did it go?" Linda asked her as she walked into the office.

"Just great! I'll tell you about it later. Is Dr. Metz in by chance?"

"He is in. Do you want me to buzz him?" Linda asked. Becca just nodded, so Linda buzzed him. "Sir, Ms. Davidson would like to talk to you if you have a moment."

"Send her in, Ms. Swartz," the intercom buzzed back.

If Becca's stomach was doing flips on the way to work, then there was a full-fledged gymnastics competition going on as she walked hesitatingly into Dr. Metz's office. Dr. John Metz had been the superintendent for almost twenty years and had been Becca's biggest supporter over the years always siding with her on safety and budget issues. So it hurt her to tell him that she would have to leave.

"Becca, have a seat," Dr. Metz said as he closed the door. The *Doctor* and *Ms.* had been set aside years ago and only when others were around did they use them today. "What can I do for you? A new bus or rebuild an old one?"

"John, I have a problem and I don't know how to handle it."

"Go ahead and tell me about it and maybe we can work something out." With that Becca began to tell him about the weekend and about the job offer.

"So you see, sir, I just don't know what to do," Becca concluded.

"Well, it looks to me that the problem is not yours, but mine," John responded.

"I don't understand."

"First of all, Dr. Houchin and I are old friends from college days. He didn't tell you that did he?" Becca shook her head. "No, probably didn't, we played rugby together at ISU. Anyway that's not important, what is, is the fact that Dwight called me Saturday night and outlined the whole proposition for me. So I knew what you wanted before you came in. I am glad that you came in here first instead of gossiping in the lounge. But then I told Dwight you would, because that is the kind of person you are. So after thinking about it all weekend, I am prepared to offer you a consulting job at your present hourly pay rate. You may work as many hours as you need or none at all. Whatever suits you best."

Becca was shocked. "I don't know what to say."

"How about thank you and how gracious of an offer," Dr. Metz replied.

"Thank you, sir, how gracious of an offer," Becca mimicked. She rose to leave and as she opened the door, Dr. Metz spoke.

"Ms. Davidson, I am proud of you. Go and make the school proud also."

"Thank you again and I really mean it." Becca told him as she exited. With that part of the transition taken care of, Becca knew she needed to head over to Moluntha State and get started.

# Chapter 5

The drive was as pleasant as it was the previous weekend, maybe even more so because Becca wasn't nearly as nervous as she had been last Saturday. Once again she marveled at the beautiful landscaping of the campus as she turned down the main drive to the building that contained the offices of the History Department. She had changed into a sensible pantsuit and put a jacket on over the white silk blouse before heading up the steps to the building.

"Becca Davidson to see Dr. Houchin." Davidson told the co-ed that was sitting at the reception desk.

"Go right on in, Ms Davidson," she said after checking an appointment book on the desk. "He said that he was expecting you and to go right to his office." Becca looked a little surprised, but followed the instructions and headed down the hall to his office. The door to his office was cracked open but Becca stopped and knocked on the frame anyway.

"Come in, Ms. Davidson, come in," Dr. Houchin rose from his desk and met her as she entered. With great enthusiasm her shook her hand and led her to one of the overstuffed chairs in front of his desk. A young lady was sitting in the chair opposite Becca's. "Would you care for a cup of coffee or tea?"

"Yes, please, a cup of tea would be fine."

"Good," he picked up the intercom and began speaking, "Sally can you get Ms. Davidson a cup of tea please. What kind? Let me check." Holding his hand over the receiver he looked at Becca and asked, "What kind would you like?"

"Earl Gray if you have some."

"Earl Gray?" he said into the receiver as both a question and statement. "You do? Very well." Looking back at Becca, "She said it would be here shortly."

"Thank you."

"I take everything was OK at your school this morning. John didn't give you any trouble, did he?"

"No, he was more than gracious."

"Good, let me introduce you to your new assistant. Pam Gibson, this is Becca Davidson. Becca meet Pam." Dr. Houchin made the introductions. Both ladies stood and shook hands. Pam was a young lady in her mid-twenties, about five feet tall, with brown hair. She was the complete opposite in build of Becca, but her bright smile sparkled like the morning sun on a lake, and Becca knew that they would get along fabulously. After the ladies returned to their seats, Dr. Houchin continued with the orientation.

"Becca, here is a packet containing the details of the program. You should find everything you need to know in order to get up and running. If you have any other questions let me know. Pam is to be your assistant and shadow; she will help you with anything you need, from typing to research. I think you will find her quite capable in her role." The professor turned to Pam. "As we talked earlier, you are to help make sure this program is a success. The program's success and your future depend upon your work. OK?"

"OK," Pam replied. The statement that Dr. Houchin had just made to Pam caused Becca to worry slightly. Were her initial thoughts wrong? Did the young lady have a hidden agenda? Becca certainly hoped not. But they would work that out later.

"I have managed to find a small office for the two of you to share.

Sally will show you where it is. If you need any equipment or supplies let her know and she will get it for you," Dr. Houchin concluded. Picking up the intercom, he buzzed Sally who appeared almost instantaneously. As they left for their new office, Dr. Houchin offered the last word of advice. "Becca, we have your first seminar scheduled for three weeks from tomorrow, so you will need to hustle."

"Thank you, I will try not to disappoint you," Becca said as she closed the door behind her. Sally led Becca and Pam down the hall and around the corner to their new office. New was a misnomer, in that it was only new to them and had nothing to do with the furnishings. The two gunmetal gray desks and chairs were cast offs from some other era, which Davidson was sure was a prehistoric era. The only new items appeared to be the two laptops and printers sitting on each of the desks. As Pam sat down in one of the chairs it squeaked and groaned so loudly that Pam jumped and Becca started laughing. It took Gibson about two seconds to join in and soon both were holding their sides with laughter.

"If we laugh like this," Gibson said in gasps between laughs, "we will never get any work done."

"I know," Becca laughed, "but somehow the thought of one of those stuffy profs sitting in a chair that bad, is just too funny."

"OK, since I made the first noise in that chair I will take that desk," Pam stated as she got her laughing under control.

"Sounds good to me. Besides I can look out the window and daydream then," Becca said as she settled into her chair, taking care not to squeak it like Pam had hers. "So tell me a little about yourself and I will do the same."

"Well let's see. I have a B.A. in history and I am a graduate student here working on my Masters. I am single, but looking, not too hard, but looking. I grew up in Nebraska just outside of Lincoln," Pam told her. "What is your story?"

"Well first of all, I am a school bus mechanic by trade." Davidson went on to relay the events of the last couple of months leading up to her sitting in this office. She also told her a little about her ex-husband and the race track and the bimbo from two counties over.

Becca related how she had raised Rachael and became a mechanic to support herself. "And like you, I am looking, but not too hard," she said as she finished her tale.

"That is amazing," Pam said as she stared at Becca. "I had no idea."

"After hearing my story and knowing that I don't have a degree," Davidson said somewhat apologetically, "are you sure you still want to work with me?"

"Absolutely, Ms. Davidson. I heard your program at the conference and was totally impressed with it. So when Dr. Houchin called and said he had an opportunity for me to be your assistant, provided of course that you accepted, which he knew you would. I jumped at the chance to work for you. Let's put it this way, if I can get a little of your love for the Old West and you can benefit from my book knowledge, together we will be a dynamite team. Fair enough?"

"Fair enough!" Becca replied. "Oh yeah, save the Ms. Davidson routine for when the profs are around. When it is just you and me it's the Becca and Pam show. Now let's see if we can get this mess organized."

The rest of the day was spent arranging and rearranging the small office. They both showed up early the next day and continued the unpacking. Finally at the end of the second day the office looked like it belonged to Becca and Pam. Pictures of buffalo, Native Americans, and John Wayne lined the walls. The shelves were filled with trinkets and books. A Navajo rug hung next to the door. This was her new home and her new life had begun.

Becca was impressed at how hard Pam worked at digging up new materials for her seminar and show. Becca reviewed the materials and adapted them to the level that most kids would enjoy. The days turned into weeks and the date for her first seminar at a nearby school was tomorrow. They had just finished packing the last of the items into the back of the Jeep, when Pam handed her a small package.

"You shouldn't have," Becca said as she opened the gift. Inside was a small dream catcher styled after the ones like the Lakota Sioux made. For a second, a chill went over Becca as she thought she saw a face in the dream catcher. She blinked and the face was gone. Had it been there she could only guess. "I love it. It is so beautiful. Did you make it?"

"Yes, I did," Pam answered. "I hope you catch your dreams in it."

"I believe I will, thank you," she said, thinking of the face she had momentarily seen in the catcher. "I believe I will."

Their first seminar was for the fourth grade class of Western Elementary in the Quad Cities. Becca and Pam arrived early and set up their table full of Sioux artifacts. There was a small glitch with the projector, but that was taken care of easily by one of the teachers. When the children were seated on the floor of the gym, Becca appeared dressed as a Plains Indian Squaw, complete with beads and moccasins. Every eye was upon her as she told of life on the Plains one hundred and fifty years ago. Using computer animation, she took them down the path that a tribe would have taken during the course of a year. After the presentation, she asked for questions and answered them until she was stopped by one of the teachers. The teachers and children all stood and applauded as she told them good bye and then doing a spirit dance, she danced her way out the door.

Finding a chair, Becca collapsed from exhaustion. She had no idea how draining it was to teach with that level of energy for two hours. Pam appeared with a bottle of cold water. Pam, as Becca had come to find out, was ever vigilant in looking out for Becca's needs. In the three weeks they had worked together, Becca had come to appreciate her diligence to her job. They sat and sipped the cold water as the children left the gym. Several of them waved to her as they walked by; many smiled slyly as if they were afraid to be noticed by a "celebrity." After the last of the children had left, Becca and Pam headed back into the gym to begin to pack things up. They were about three quarters of the way loaded when the principal walked up to them and extended her hand.

"I just wanted to let you know that I really enjoyed your presentation today," the principal commented. "I walked in at the beginning just to make sure everything was OK and got caught up in it and stayed the whole time. Tell me how long have you been doing this?"

Giant smiles spread across their faces. Becca looked down at her watch and as seriously as she could, she looked back up and replied, "Would you believe about two and a half hours?"

"You're kidding me, really how long have you been doing this?"

"Honestly, this is the first time. Up until three weeks ago I was a bus mechanic and Pam was working on her Master's degree." Becca grinned.

"I never would have guessed. It was fantastic. We will schedule you again in the spring for the whole elementary. Thank you so much for your teaching." The principal shook their hands one more time and then left. Within ten minutes the Cherokee was loaded and they were on their way back to the university.

"You know, Pam, this could get to be really fun," Becca commented as they sped down the freeway.

"I understand fully," Pam replied, "except for one thing—it's fun already."

"Yeah, you can say that again." Becca laughed and Pam joined in. The trip back to the university was relaxing. Both Pam and Becca talked about what went right and what they could improve on. Dr. Houchin was waiting for them in their office when they returned.

"So how did it go?" the professor inquired.

"Great, it was absolutely fantastic," Becca said with the same enthusiasm that she had when she spoke. For the next hour the two of them recounted the morning at the elementary school. It was long after five when they finished talking and Dr. Houchin quit asking questions.

"Thank you for your work, Ms. Davidson and Ms. Gibson. The department is proud of the work that you have done. Now if you ladies will excuse me I would like to go home to Mrs. Houchin and some supper." With those final words, Dr. Houchin stood and left the room. Becca and Pam looked at each other for a second, grabbed their coats and headed out the door.

"You thinking what I'm thinking?" Becca asked Pam as they walked across the parking lot toward their vehicles.

"Yeah, this calls for a celebration. You call Rachael and have her us meet at the Cork and Cleaver," Pam said.

"Gotcha, I'll meet you there in ten minutes." Becca climbed into the Cherokee and dug her cell phone out of her purse. The number was in her directory so she speed dialed and waited for someone to answer.

"Hello, this is Rachael," her daughter's voice chimed as she answered the phone.

"Hey Rach, this is Mom."

"How did it go today?"

"Great...."

"Tell me all about it, Mom."

"If you will be quiet for five seconds I will."

"Sorry," Rachael apologized.

"That's OK. It went great. Pam and I are going out. Do you want to join us?" Becca asked.

"Sure it beats housesitting while you are out running around. Where to?"

"The Cork and Cleaver. In fifteen minutes."

"This IS going to be a celebration. Let me change and I will be right over. See you there." Rachael hung up the phone. The Cork and Cleaver was one of the nicer pubs in the Quad Cities and the place to be if you really wanted to celebrate. Boasting the finest wine cellar and the best beef in four counties, the inn drew people from as far away as Chicago. With such an upscale clientele, one didn't have to worry too much about any bar fights taking place.

Pam was waiting at the door when Becca arrived. She had already put their name in with the hostess. "It is about a twenty minute wait for a table, do you want to wait in the bar?

"If you don't mind, let's stay out here and wait on Rach," Davidson suggested.

"Fine with me." The two ladies settled onto the bench that ran alongside the wall. No sooner than they had sat down, the door opened and in walked Rachael. Becca jumped up and gave her daughter a hug.

"Wow, you look great tonight. I feel grossly underdressed all of a sudden," Becca commented. Not that Becca Davidson had anything to worry about. Whenever she went out in public she always looked great, and tonight was no exception, the black pin-striped slacks and light blue silk blouse looked fantastic and were turning the guys' heads left and right. But she was right that her daughter was a knockout tonight, in a black mini skirt and gray striped turtleneck sweater. Pam had chosen a dark blue cocktail mini dress, and with her high-heeled sandals, she was getting her share of looks.

Rachael had just checked her coat when the hostess said that their table was ready. The Cork and Clever Inn's main dining area was set around a dance floor and small bandstand. Each night from seven to close a local jazz band would play and people would dance. The trio's table was located on the far side of the dance floor and Pam felt just a little self-conscious as the eyes followed them to their seats.

"I would like to recommend the grilled salmon tonight," the hostess said as she handed each a menu. "I'll be up front if you need me. Your server will be here shortly to take your order." True to her word, their server showed up almost immediately to take their drink orders.

"I think I will have a glass of white wine," Pam told the waiter.

"That sounds great, I'll have one also," Becca said.

"Make that three," Rach chimed in. The server left to get the drinks. "So I am dying to know, how did it go today?"

"Oh it was great. You should have seen your mom, she was just fantastic," Pam started, but Becca interrupted.

"I had so much fun, the kids were just glued to me watching everything I did," Becca continued. Soon Pam and Becca were telling her about the presentation and the rest of the day, stopping only to order their meal.

Becca ordered the grilled salmon with grilled vegetables. Pam said that she would have a chicken breast and fries. Rach decided on the ribeye steak and a baked potato. As soon as the waiter set the last of the plates on the table and left, the conversation continued. Finally Pam turned to Rachael and asked how her day was.

"Pretty good actually. The company was asked to help design a major presentation for one of the auto parts suppliers and my boss, Marty, asked me to head it up."

"Well then, Pam and I aren't the only ones celebrating tonight," Becca said raising her wine glass. "A toast to three ladies whose ships have finally arrived." The glasses clinked and the women giggled.

At exactly seven o'clock, the little jazz ensemble got on the stage and began to play. The band was playing smooth jazz and the dance floor began to fill up. Gibson sipped a little more wine and tapped her feet to the rhythm, wondering if anyone would ask them to dance, and if she would have the nerve to say yes. Pam didn't have to wait long for her answer, about halfway through the second song, two guys wandered up to the table.

"Excuse me, I was wondering if you would like to dance?" the taller of the two asked. He was looking at Rachael, but it was obvious that he was speaking for them both and that the other guy was looking at Pam. Rachael looked over at her mom and Becca gave her that slight nod as if to say she would be fine.

"I, for one, would love to dance," said Pam. She had picked up on the nod from Becca and was going to enjoy the evening. "My name is Pam, this is Becca and Rachael." She pointed to each of the ladies as she spoke.

"My name is Chris and this is Eric." It was the shorter of the two's turn to speak as he took Pam's hand. He and Eric led the ladies to the dance floor as the band picked up the pace with a New Orleans style jazz number. Chris was a good dancer and Pam was enjoying herself and as she glanced over at Rach, she could tell she was also. Pam wondered about Becca, but couldn't see her from the dance floor. Just then Chris took her hand, gave her a twirl and all thoughts of Becca left Pam's mind.

Becca sat at their table thinking that she was going to be the old maid tonight and would wind up drinking too much and getting obnoxious. She took a long sip of her wine and wondered if Jack Daniels might taste better. She let her mind drift back to her younger days when she and Frank had danced the nights away, closing down clubs as they celebrated after a race. The jazz beat slowed down into a sultry blues number and it seemed to match Becca's mood perfectly. So absorbed was she in feeling sorry for herself that she didn't notice the man that came up and sat down in one of the vacant chairs and when he spoke, she just about screamed.

"Penny for your thoughts," the smooth baritone voice asked. After he saw her jump, he quickly apologized, "I am so sorry I didn't mean to startle you. May I pour you some more wine?"

Becca took a huge breath before answering, "No thank you. I think I have had enough for tonight."

"OK, then may I introduce myself," the man said, extending his hand. "My name is Mark."

"Nice to meet you, Mark," she said, accepting his offered hand. "On better days I am called Becca, tonight call me Gloomy."

"I like Becca better," Mark replied. "To invoke an old saying and risked getting slapped, what is a lovely lady like you doing sitting alone on a night like this?"

"Number one," Becca said smiling, "I am not alone because my two friends are on the dance floor. And number two, it is because no one has asked me to dance."

"I can remedy part two. Would you care to dance?"

The warning bells were sounding inside of Becca's head as she thought over his request. There was something just a little too smooth and too practiced in his pick up lines to be real. Every part of her brain was telling her to say no, but her lonely heart was screaming yes. The lonely heart won and she said yes. They rose and walked to the dance floor. Becca took the time to look at Mark. He was just over six feet, a little thin boned, but that was better than being "big boned." While Becca could fast dance with the best of them, she was glad that the jazz band was still playing a slow, smooth jazz number. Taking Mark's hand she moved into position and let him lead the way. Mark wasn't a bad dancer and the blues quickly left Becca. After three songs though, it was time to sit down and give Becca a chance to catch her breath. Reluctantly, Mark conceded and led her back to the table. Back at the table Mark ordered a beer and Becca another glass of wine. They made small talk for a little while until Rach, Pam, Chris, and Eric made their way back to the table.

"You're a great dancer," Eric said to Pam after they had all caught their breath.

"Oh flattery will get you everywhere," Pam replied. For the next hour the six sat together and talked. Each couple took turns dancing and flirting. It was one of the times that Becca and Mark were out on the dance floor that Chris spoke up.

"Rach, I don't know if I am the one that should bring this up," he began, somewhat hesitantly, "but I like your mother and I think she needs to know that Mark isn't all he seems to be."

"What do you mean?" Rach asked. The comment caught Pam's attention also.

"Maybe I should just let it play itself out and not interfere," Chris said, wishing he had never brought up the subject.

"You opened the door, now finish it," Rach said.

Eric looked at Chris seriously and said, "Look, Chris, if you don't tell them I will."

"Well it's like this, I know for a fact that he is married and has at least one on the side," Chris said, not at all happy with himself. Once he got started though, he couldn't stop. "Rumor has also that he leaves here every weekend with another woman. Becca seems nice enough and from what you have told me she doesn't need hurt right now."

Rachael was shaking with anger as she stood up and looked over at the man with her mom. If Chris and Pam hadn't grabbed her arms, she would have been on her way to a good, old-fashioned bar brawl. The three of them managed to get her halfway calmed down by the time the song ended and Mark was leading Becca back for another drink. Eric took Rachael's arm and headed her toward the dance floor. Pam looked at Becca and said she needed to go to the girl's room. Together they headed toward the restrooms.

"We gotta talk," Pam said, distress showing in her voice.

"What's wrong?" Becca replied. "Eric or Chris not acting with honorable intentions?"

"No, it's Mark," Pam said, waiting for the infamous Rebecca

Davidson temper to erupt. But it didn't and after Pam had finished telling her everything that Eric and Chris had told her about Mark, she waited for Mount St. Helens to blow. Instead Becca just smiled.

"Thanks, I kinda figured just as much. My jerk alert has been on overload since he said hi. So I guess I will have to learn to trust it more," her smile getting bigger as she spoke.

"You have that look, Becca."

"What look?"

"You know," Pam said with a smile, "the look that says I am going to scalp me a white man."

"Who me? Never," Becca replied mockingly. "I promise no blood or bruises, but he may wish he was scalped." With those words Becca turned and walked out of the restroom with Pam in tow. As they walked, Pam noticed Becca's gait change, from a confident lady to that of a sexy tramp, the very plaything Mark was looking for. With a sexy crook of her finger, Becca motioned for him to follow her to the dance floor. The ensemble was playing a quick Latin-sounding number and Becca continued her act by teasing him with her dance.

"What is she doing?" Eric asked as he watched her heat up the dance floor and Mark. "You did tell her, didn't you?"

"I told her," Pam said, "and all she said was she promised no blood." The four continued to watch as Becca tempted and teased him with her dance moves. Pam caught a few steps that looked an awful lot like a Sioux war dance, but she didn't say anything to the others. Finally the dance ended and Becca led Mark back to the table. Mark was so obviously ready to take Becca away that he didn't notice her wink at Pam and Rachael.

"You know, maybe we ought to leave these kids alone," Becca cooed, running her finger alongside of his face. Mark's breathing was shallow and fast, but the next words stopped his breath altogether. "I know the preacher at the Methodist church and he could marry us tonight."

"Wwwhhaaaat?" Mark stammered. It was all the other four could do to keep straight faces. Mark was out of his league and he didn't know it. Rachael caught on to the game and chimed in.

"Oh, the Episcopalian priest does a much better job, and he is cheaper too," Rach said in a voice that mimicked her mother's. "I hope he don't die as quick as your last one." Turning to Eric, she put her hand to her face but didn't lower her voice. "He committed suicide after three days. Anyway that is the 'official story' Mother gave the police."

"Suicide? Police?" Mark said, all arousal was gone, only fear shown in his eyes. Quickly he slid his chair back. "Would you look at the time? I have a flight to catch. It was nice meeting you!"

"So quickly? I can have the preacher here in five minutes," Becca suggested.

"That is five minutes I don't have." With those words he left, almost running for the door. Instantly, the five remaining at the table burst into a chorus of laughter. It was Chris who spoke first, still holding his side laughing.

"Did…you…see…his…face? It…was…pure…terror." The words came out in between spasms of laughter. Pam was a little calmer when she spoke.

Looking at Rachael, she asked, "Did you two rehearse that? It was great. Suicide in three days? What a riot." The rest of the evening was spent laughing at Mark's expense. Just a look or comment about anything remotely related to him and they all started laughing again. When the show ended, the three ladies and two men left the bar together. Chris and Eric said goodnight to Pam and Rachael. The ladies gave them their phone numbers, accepted quick kisses on their cheeks and said goodbye. Joining back up with Becca they laughed and giggled at each other as they headed across the parking lot to their vehicles. Rachael gave her mother a hug good night and drove off for Eagleton. Pam was in her Pontiac and gone shortly after. Becca followed the others out of the drive. When she pulled her Jeep into the driveway at her townhouse, she felt a strangeness come over her. It was almost as if someone was beside her. Blaming it on the wine, she walked into the house, carefully checking the corners as she went. She dropped her purse by the door and headed down the hall for her bedroom, when she came to a stop. Slowly she turned and looked over in the corner of the room where she had hung the dream catcher that Pam had given her. In the center there appeared to be a face of a man in it. Slowly she walked through the dimly lit room. As she got close enough to see the catcher clearly, the face disappeared.

"I feel like Ebenezer Scrooge with pictures of Jacob Marley on the door," Becca said to herself as left the living room and went to bed. Sleep didn't come easy for her, so about three in the morning she got up and made herself some hot tea. The warmth relaxed her and she wondered where she had gone wrong with her love life. The feelings of joy from earlier in the evening had been replaced by loneliness. She knew it wasn't any fault of hers that her ex-husband, Frank, had gotten friendly with a waitress over in another town. He had carried on the affair for almost two years, while she was home raising a daughter, and then one day he decided not to come home and moved in with her.

*It wasn't my fault,* she thought as she sipped her tea.

"It wasn't my fault," she repeated out loud as she looked again at the dream catcher and tried to erase the lonely feeling that was welling up inside her. It was a feeling she had kept at bay for many years with wit and a sharp tongue. One by one tears began to stream from her eyes, slowly breaking through the wall of resistance that she had so carefully constructed. Sobs came as Becca cried for the first time in a long time as the hurts of the last fifteen years poured from her soul. Tears, some say, have a cleansing effect and one by one washed away the pain, until exhausted, Becca fell asleep on the chair dreaming of the face in the dream catcher.

# Chapter 6

Life for Roy was anything but living; there were those brief moments when it felt like he was living, like dinner with the Mitchell's or at Kilkenny's. The firm kept him busy; there was always a deal to make or a crisis to manage. Win or lose there was always a fee to be billed and that is what kept the wheels of commerce turning. Roy did enjoy the process, but he could never forget what Wendy said to Peter Pan in the movie *Hook* when he told her what he did. "Why Peter, you have become a pirate." And sometimes Roy Curtis felt like a pirate.

The northern Indiana snows and the short daylight hours kept Roy from spending very much quality time at the farm. Two things kept Curtis from going crazy in the winter months. The first was the coed volleyball league that he and Sheridan played in at the club around the corner from the office. The second was his monthly obligation to his government, drill weekend with the Reserves.

The second weekend of each month, Roy left work early and headed for a weekend of Reserve duty at the Great Lakes Naval Base. Roy was the executive officer of a reserve Marine Expeditionary Unit. Stationed also with the MEU headquarters was a logistics company.

Lt. Col. Curtis had been promoted to his present position two years ago. The company was charged with maintaining the supply containers and the motor pool for the 4$^{th}$ Force Service Support Group, the main supply unit for the United States Marine Corp Reserve based out of New Orleans.

Lt. Col Curtis changed from his suit and tie into his desert camouflaged uniform and drove to Lake Michigan. He slowed at the main gate, so the Shore Patrolman could see his sticker, snap a salute and wave him through. Curtis returned the salute and headed to the headquarters building. Straightening his uniform as he walked to the entrance, Roy couldn't help but think of the months he had spent in the Gulf during the first war. Faces of the men he had served with, the wounded, and the dead passed in front of his eyes, thoughts that filled him with sorrow. The sorrow was quickly replaced with pride as he remembered the selfless and daring acts that they had accomplished during those days.

"Good afternoon, Top. Anything new happening this weekend?" Curtis asked the First Sergeant, who was working on the duty board as he walked into the office. First Sergeant Edward Holycross had been with the MEU since before Curtis joined the unit. A compact Marine with a bundle of energy, the First Sergeant commanded both fear and respect among the enlisted troops. Heaven help the Marine that failed to make roll call on time. Holycross was also the MEU champion marksman; he was deadly at any distance with just about any firearm in the arsenal.

"Not much, sir. Colonel Kilkenny wants to work on exercise planning this weekend. He called and said he would be here in about a half an hour."

"Good," Curtis replied, "let me get a glass of iced tea and we will get to work. Any personnel problems this weekend?"

"Nothing too critical, Lance Corporal Henderson's wife is having a baby and he is over at the Naval Hospital. Other than that everyone is accounted for."

Roy headed into his office and opened the large thermos he had brought with him. Taking out an old thirty-two ounce McDonald's glass, he filled it with ice and poured it full of tea. Picking up his notebook and laptop he headed for the conference room. Because they were a reserve unit instead of a regular MEU, most of the exercise planning was done for them at the Force headquarters in New Orleans. The exception was the small squad and platoon level exercises that they did during the weekend drills. There were about a dozen officers and staff non-commissioned officers scattered about the conference when Roy got there. Someone rose to announce him as the senior officer, but Curtis quickly waved him off. The reserve MEU was as close a band of brothers as any in the Fleet Marine Force and most of the time they spoke as brothers, respecting the rank, but relaxing the protocol when possible. Curtis sat the large plastic glass and notebook on the table and made his way around the room greeting his fellow weekend warriors.

"Well if this isn't a motley bunch," Curtis said with a grin as he approached a group sitting in the back corner. "Top, couldn't you find someplace better to sit with than this bunch of losers?"

"No, sir, I couldn't, and it sure don't say much for the leadership around here, does it?" Top Holycross gave a huge smile as he replied.

"Good afternoon, Gunny, Gunner." Curtis extended his hand to each as they rose. Gunnery Sergeant Isaiah Washington stood six foot three inches and weighed closed to two hundred and thirty pounds. Besides being the Unit's kick boxing champ, the gunny prided himself at being the electronics whiz kid of the unit. If it was the latest and greatest in computers, PDA's or communication devices, then Washington knew all there was to know about it. Next to him was Chief Warrant Officer 4 Rafael Ramirez; Ramirez was the resident expert in hand-to-hand combat and trained most of the officers in the room the finer points of knife fighting as only a kid from the south side could. That in itself wasn't so unusual except when you added it to his primary occupational specialty, which was that of a pilot. The gunner could fly any rotary wing aircraft in the corps and most of the fixed wings. Curtis had commented more than once that more than half of the unit owed their lives to these three, and if the count were ever made, it was probably closer to three quarters.

"Attention on deck!" someone shouted and instantly with Pavlovian reflexes, everyone was on his feet and standing at attention. The Commanding Officer, Colonel John P. Kilkenny USMCR, entered the room and looked at his staff. Like Lt. Col. Curtis, he waved the staff at ease and took his seat at the head of the table. Curtis first met Kilkenny when he was serving his initial duty station at Camp Pendleton, California. The then 1st Lt. Kilkenny was the S3 training officer and 2nd Lt. Curtis had just been assigned as the S4 logistics officer for the 1/7 Marines. They formed a fast friendship and served together in the Gulf War. Both were glad to be working together in this Reserve MEU. Colonel John Patrick Kilkenny was a stereotypical Irishmen. The tall, broad-shouldered man with his flame red hair cropped short looked the part of a military officer and probably would have captained a man-of-war schooner had he been born in the 1800's. Kilkenny was a very good officer and would have been awarded a star for his flag had he elected to stay on active duty.

"OK, gentlemen, let's get to work, so we can have some fun," Kilkenny said, looking at the training agenda. "Let's start with the Company level exercises and work our way down the list." With that, the officers and NCOs began to put the final touches on the exercises they would be running through during the unit's two-week summer camp. Make a plan. Check the plan. Execute the plan. That was Colonel Kilkenny's creed and that's what they lived by. So they talked about objectives, targets, troop movements, weapons, food and fuel for each exercise. One by one each exercise was planned, a date assigned to it and what unit would be involved. When they got down to the last of the small unit exercises, Gunner Ramirez spoke up.

"Colonel, we have already assigned each squad an insertion exercise. What do you want to do with this one? It looks like another squad insertion."

"Why don't we make it a cold weather aerial insertion exercise?" someone with a voice that sounded like the Top's hollered. Everyone laughed, because that meant the Gunner would have to flight it and they all knew how cold a helicopter was.

"Sounds great to me," the CO replied, "and the squad with the lowest proficiency score gets to join him." Those words quieted the room because each of them had at least one squad that would be in the contest and none of them wanted to be flying around in helicopter during a Midwestern snowstorm.

"Anything else?" Kilkenny asked as he closed his notebook. Everyone shook their head in the negative and the meeting was adjourned, with all the work finished for the weekend, Colonel Kilkenny led the way his office where the fun would begin.

The monthly poker game had become a tradition for the five veterans of the Gulf War. Each took up his regular position, the Colonel sat in his desk chair, to his right was Top Holycross, Gunny Washington sat on a wooden stool that threaten to break under his large frame. Lt Col Curtis sat across from Kilkenny in the chair from his office and Gunner Ramirez sat in the visitor's chair to complete the table. The game was a penny ante game with each only allowed to lose a maximum of ten dollars. Keeping the stakes low kept the five as friends, but still they were serious about the game.

They played five-card draw, no fancy high stakes hold 'em, just good old-fashioned poker. It was the kind of card game where lives, women and work were discussed and a lot of food consumed. Each had their own style. Washington was the flamboyant trash talker, always bragging about how good his hand was even if it was just a ten high hand. Rafe like to fidget, always twirling his ring or shuffle his hand from front to back and back again. The master sergeant played with his chips, picking them up and letting them fall. Kilkenny and Curtis could have been cut from the same piece of granite when it came to reading them. Neither moved except to add chips to the pot until they were sure of a winning hand and then the smile that would have made Maverick proud spread across the winner's face while the other would pout in mock disgust.

As they played the conversation turned from topic to topic finally back to the one unassigned exercise. Gunner broached the subject with care as not to risk the anger of the CO. Kilkenny's red hair was a good indicator of the potential wrath that could come from crossing him. After the Colonel had won a couple of hands, the Gunner asked the question.

"Sir, you weren't serious about that cold weather exercise?"

"As serious as a heart attack," Kilkenny replied, but everyone could see him trying not to smile. After the appropriate pregnant pause, the Colonel broke out his signature smile. "Oh the exercise will go on, but when and who is a different question. Let's call it Cold Blitz and mark the date TBA." With that settled the game continued well into the night. They seemed to lose all sense of time when they were playing, so the game was still going strong when the first rays of daylight peaked over Lake Michigan. That is when common sense took over and they called the game quits. The five packed away the chips for another month and headed to the mess hall for breakfast with the rest of the troops.

Curtis and Kilkenny both loaded their trays full and sat down at the end of the officer's table. Neither said much as they concentrated on using the food to knock the cobwebs from their brains.

"These eggs aren't too bad today," Roy commented, "must have used real eggs."

Kilkenny laughed and poured a little more Tabasco sauce on his eggs. Military chow was the same around the world and even a presidential decree couldn't change that fact.

"Say why don't you come over for supper on Tuesday?" Kilkenny asked. "Catherine has been wanting you to come over."

"Can't on Tuesday, that's volleyball night. How about Thursday?" Curtis replied.

"Thursday night around 6:30 it is then," Kilkenny confirmed.

The Van Buren Health and Fitness Club was made up of mostly young professionals that worked in the area. From nine to five the club was almost deserted, but every morning from five a.m. until eight the place was packed with those people trying to stay in shape. The same thing rang true in the evening with men and women working out the stress of the day with the clang of weights and the whir of the treadmills and lifecycles. Mike and Roy were regulars there during the winter months.

The volleyball league was made up of teams consisting of members of the health clubs. The teams were formed at random, but tended to follow occupations of the members. The lawyers and paralegals fielded three different teams, with accountants, bankers and brokers each having a team apiece. The league was supposed to be for fun and bragging rights only, but most of the teams took their bragging rights seriously, so the competition and play were fierce. Mike and Roy had formed the Ninth Street Raiders from staff members of their investment and commercial banks. They were a solid team and always finished high in the league standings.

Tonight they were scheduled to play the Bottom Feeders, one of the law teams. The Bottom Feeders were just ahead of the Raiders in the standings and it promised to be a good match. All ten members of the team were present tonight and ready to play. That in itself was unusual as someone was always away on a business trip or in a meeting. It also meant that they could give a couple of the players who were nursing injuries a break and let them sit out unless absolutely needed. Mike had recruited the other investment banking firms to find the other members, with one exception, and that was Jane Riggs.

Jane Riggs was a commodities trader on the floor of the Chicago Board of Trade. Roy had met her about six years ago at an agricultural conference in Indianapolis. They had been seated next to each other during a panel discussion on financial risk management. The session had been running behind schedule so they were late getting back to the airport, when it became obvious that Riggs would not get through security in time to catch her flight, Curtis had graciously offered to allow her to join him on the firm's jet back to Chicago. During the flight home they had gotten to know each other. Roy had told her briefly about his background, including the death of Jacki and Brent. It turned out that Jane had attended Purdue and had been a starter for their volleyball team. Being the ever-diligent scout, Curtis had promptly recruited her to play for the team. With Riggs on the team, the Ninth Street Raiders had gone from being just another team to being a contender for the league title.

Sheridan served as coach for the Raiders and did a fairly decent job of rotating players in and out of the match. Besides taking advantage of player's skills, it also gave the older players a much-needed breather. Since Roy was a decent server, he had developed three different serves over the years; he started in the corner serving. Jane was the team setter with Mike and Steve Walters doing the spiking and blocking duties. The Bottom Feeders had their share of ringers also. Two of their players, Ross Barker and Heath Carter, had played volleyball in college and could have played on the professional circuit if they had wanted.

The Bottom Feeders served first and after a good volley, Heath blocked one of Mike's spikes and scored first blood. Then a side out and it was Roy's turn to serve. Riggs had helped him develop a rocket jump serve, which he promptly delivered for an ace as it careened off of a player's arm. Mixing it up he served a knuckle ball no spin that they returned but Steve blocked. By the time Curtis was done serving, the score was four to one in favor of the Raiders. With a couple of slams by Carter and some great serves by Barker, the Feeders fought back to win the first game 16 to 14. The second game was revenge time and the Raiders shut out the attorneys fifteen to zip.

The final game of the match was pretty even each side trading serves and points. The Bottom Feeders had managed to pull ahead and were leading by one. The Feeders busted the Raiders serve and were now set up to win the game and match. The serve was a power serve that rocketed across the court just clearing the net and dropping fast. Jane was in the back row and made a diving save to her left. The ball popped up to the front row and Sheridan set the ball high near the net. As the ball dropped Barker jumped and slammed the ball toward the far right corner. For an instant the Raiders thought the ball had landed inside the base line. Then the line judge lifted his flag and signaled the ball had hit the line and that the point, game and match belonged to the Bottom Feeders. A collective groan emerged from the Ninth Street Raiders as the team members sank to their knees or buried their heads in their hands in despair.

Shaking his head in disbelief, Roy made his way to the net and congratulated the victors. It was going to be a long winter if it was filled with close calls and losses. He could only hope that this was not a signal of things to come at work and the farm.

Thursday rolled around quickly and Roy found himself scrambling to get his work finished before heading over to the Kilkenny's for dinner. It was a quick trip north to the slate gray colonial house that John and Jessica called home. It was in one of the older neighborhoods, not one of those fancy gated communities that had sprung up all over the outskirts of the city. As the Z4 slipped past the wrought iron gates that stood guard on the Colonel's home, Curtis felt like he had been transported back to an older time.

Jessica opened the large oaken door before Roy had a chance to ring the doorbell and welcomed him in. Jessica Lynn Kilkenny was the perfect picture of a Marine Corps Officer's wife, proper and polite in her manners. She was wearing a periwinkle cashmere sweater, a single strand of pearls and black pinstriped wool slacks. The calfskin boots with three inch heals brought up closer to John Patrick's height and her short black hair made her look even taller.

"Come in Roy," she welcomed him in. "It is so good to see you, what has it been three or four months? It doesn't matter, I am just glad that you are here." Jess reached up and gave Roy a big hug. "JP's in the den, dinner will be ready in a few minutes."

Curtis walked down the center hall to the den, a quick knock and then he pushed back the sliding pocket door and entered the den. If he thought he had traveled back in time when he passed through the front gate, Roy was sure of it when he entered the den. Den was the modern word, a library or study would have been a better name. The walls were lined with solid dark cherry shelves. About half of the shelves were devoted to books of every subject, but most were on the military in one fashion or another. In a prominent position was a series of books by the late, great Ohio State University football coach, Woody Hayes, who, besides being a great coach, was a professor of military history.

The rest of the shelving was filled with military artifacts and awards. On the left side was the sword that General Grant had used during the Civil War. A musket from a Confederate Marine hung above it. On the right side was a World War II campaign hat that John's dad had worn when he served as a China Marine.

"Brandy?" John Patrick asked. Roy nodded to the affirmative, so his host took a bottle out of the cabinet and poured a generous amount into a snifter and handed it to Curtis.

"To those who didn't come home," Roy offered as a toast as he held up his glass and the faces of fallen comrades flashed through his mind. Together they drank the brandy and let the distilled liquor burn as it traveled down to their stomachs.

"So how are things going?" Kilkenny inquired.

"Not too bad. A lot of the same," Curtis replied. "I am working on helping finance an expedition to dig up some old Indian village out in the Badlands. Not really my cup of tea, but Lescowitch insisted, so I do. Actually it is a favor to one of our larger clients; the owner grew up in South Dakota and had heard stories of the village from his grandma who was one quarter Sioux."

"Sounds risky," John commented in a tone that was obviously fishing for more info.

"It is a little, but the fees will be worth it and if it doesn't pan out our client will make good on the loan. He just doesn't want to put his company's cash flow at risk if possible." Just then Jessica slid opened the door and announced dinner was ready.

The dining room was as elegant as the den. A large oak fireplace with an ornate mantel dominated the far wall and the dark table could be extended to seat twelve people if needed. On the side walls hung pewter oil lamp sconces. A white linen table cloth graced the table and the china and silverware dated back to the late 1700's.

Jess had fixed broiled trout and asparagus spears. The white wine was excellent and the trio of friends emptied the decanter as they ate and talked. John and Roy did most of the talking while Jessica listened and interjected as needed. Dinner was over and the evening was waning when the subject of the Indian village resurfaced.

"What do the diggers plan to do if they find anything?" John asked.

"Well from what I understand, there is a museum on the west side of the city that is willing to display any find and even help set up a tour for it."

"Better hand me a shovel then." The effects of the wine were beginning to show and John wobbled just a little as he walked with Roy to the door.

"You couldn't dig a good outhouse," Roy laughed at him. "We had better call in the Seabees." Roy made his way to the Beamer and hoped that he could make it home safely.

It was on a Monday afternoon when Paul Lescowitch walked into Curtis' office and sat down. He had that look in his eyes that usually meant more money for the company and more work for Roy's group. It was the same look he had had when they organized the takeover of the Twin Rivers Packing Company. Roy put the reports he had been studying down and waited for the senior partner to begin.

"I got a call from Kelly Foster today," Lescowitch said matter-of-factly. Kelly was the president and CEO of Foster Plating, Inc. and the man who had talked Paul into financing the archeology expedition into the Badlands to excavate a Sioux winter village. Curtis sighed, figuring the Foster Expedition had gone broke and was defaulting on its loan or needed more money at the best.

"They hit the mother lode of Sioux artifacts," Paul continued. This caused Curtis to catch his breath out of excitement and not dread. "They have sold the large pieces to a museum and are lending the rest for an exhibit they want to host. The grand opening is set for the second weekend in June."

"OK, what's the catch, Paul? You have that look in your eyes."

"No catch, except they have invited us to the opening and we are all going." The emphasis was on the word *all*.

"You know how I detest…," Roy began.

"Sorry," Paul interrupted. "Kelly has requested us and specifically you to attend, so attend you will, end of discussion. Besides he is too good of a client to disappoint now. Mrs. Peterson will have your invitation." Paul rose from the Queen Anne chair and walked from the office.

"Nuts," was all Curtis could think to say. "Well I guess I had better clear my calendar and get my tuxedo cleaned."

# Chapter 7

The next several months were hectic for Becca and Pam, the University kept them busy teaching and researching. Chris had called Pam and they had had dinner a couple of times since the night at the Cork and Cleaver. Rachael had stopped by and had told them that she and Eric were a steady item. Together Becca and Pam had authored three articles for magazines and research journals. Their reputation as skilled communicators was growing and the demand for them by the schools kept them away at least three nights a week. Becca hadn't had a lonely spell for a while, but the vision of the face in the dream catcher was occurring more often and slowly she began to think that she could almost make out the features.

They arrived back at the office late one spring afternoon to find a message that Dr. Houchin wanted to see them tomorrow morning at eight o'clock. Pam and Becca looked at each other and shrugged, Dr. Houchin for the most part had left the two ladies alone to develop the program as they saw fit. The request that he wanted to see both of them at the same time was the cause of a raised eyebrow or two.

"Maybe it has something to do with a summer program?" Pam speculated. "I really hope not, because the Rockies are calling me and

I want to do some serious hiking."

"I know what you mean," Davidson replied nodding her head, "as much as I enjoyed this last year, I am looking forward to a break."

"Hey, you said you fished didn't you?" Gibson asked as the light turned on inside her head.

"Yeah, I fly-fish, but it has been several years since I have been. Why?"

"I just had a thought. How about we wrap up the school year next week and go fly-fishing up in the Dells the week after that?"

"That sounds great. We could camp and sleep out under the stars like the Native Americans we teach about used to do."

"Sounds like a plan to me, but let's take a tent in case it rains. I am getting excited just thinking about it," Pam said. "But of course we could end up being unemployed after our meeting tomorrow with Dr. Houchin."

"Why do you have to be such a realist, Pam?"

"Just my destiny, I guess."

Both of the ladies were waiting outside of Dr. Houchin's office when he arrived at seven forty-five the next morning. He flung his coat over the back of a chair and motioned the ladies into his office. Becca was somewhat relieved that he didn't shut the door behind them, that meant it was either going to be quick or he didn't care who heard it. Experience told her that important meetings did not occur with the door open.

"Have a seat, please." Dr. Houchin motioned to the sofa and he pulled an overstuffed chair around to face them. "I would offer you some coffee but I see we are the first ones here this morning. I will be brief and to the point. The department is ecstatic with your work this school year and I know you would like to take some time off this summer. You both deserve it, but I am afraid that won't be possible." He took out two envelopes and handed one to Becca and the other to Pam. "Unfortunately, I have to break this great team up for a couple of weeks to get everything accomplished that needs to be done. So first of all, Pam, you will be heading into the Rockies and the western high plains and spending two weeks with a team from Colorado State studying the Shoshone Indians. The results of your studies will be published and presented at our conference next fall."

"Thank you, sir," Pam acknowledged humbly. She knew it was an honor to be asked and given the opportunity to be on the list of speakers at the conference.

"I am sorry I don't have anything quite as exciting for you," Dr Houchin said as he turned toward Becca, "but it is equally as important. I want you to teach a month-long summer session on the Native American lifestyle. I know you don't have a degree, but I do have a little pull and besides it will be just an expanded version of what you are doing in the schools now. Any questions?"

"Just the typical ones, Where? When? And how?" Becca asked.

"One question at a time Ms. Davidson." Dr. Houchin took a deep breath and began. "Where? The course will be right here at the University. 'When' is three Tuesdays from now and the 'how' part is your problem. It is a continuing education course, so you will be teaching many of the same teachers that you gave programs to this last school year. It will last for four weeks and then begin all over again. You should have time to do some research this summer also. Oh, one more thing before you go, I am sure you have read about the discovery of the Sioux tribe winter village in the Badlands. I managed to get you an invitation to the opening of a museum exhibit next weekend in Chicago that will be displaying the artifacts. It will be a great evening for you to network and learn."

"I just read about it last week," Becca replied. "Pam, it's too bad that you can't come with me, but someone has to go off with the college guys into the middle of nowhere. Come to think of it, do you want to trade places?"

"No, thanks. I think the mountains sound just fine." Pam turned to Dr. Houchin. "Thank you so much for everything you have done for us. Ms. Davidson and I really appreciate it."

"You're welcome," Dr. Houchin said. The meeting was obviously over with the saying of those two words. The two ladies excused themselves and headed to their office.

"Well, so much for camping and fly-fishing next week," Pam said as she sank down into her chair.

"I just had an idea. Let's go this weekend. We finish at noon Friday and can be in the Dells before dark and we don't have a presentation until Tuesday."

"But what about work?"

"We will let Sharon know we are on a 'research' assignment and she can reach us by cell phone if she needs to," Becca answered, getting excited about the prospect of camping and fishing. "Do you have any idea how long it has been since I have been camping?"

"Probably about as long as it has been for me," Pam answered. "It will be a good chance to field test my gear before I go out with the boys from CSU."

"Sounds good to me. Pam, bring your gear and we will leave from here as soon as we are done with the presentation."

It had taken Becca about an hour to dig out from the top of the garage the tube that contained her fly rods and reels. Then she made a quick trip to the sporting goods store to buy new flies and line. Becca rushed into the house and packed a duffle bag with a few clothes, loaded the Cherokee and headed for Gibson's house. Pam was waiting outside with a pile of camping gear when Becca pulled in the drive. Quickly they unloaded Davidson's stuff and reloaded the all the equipment. Within fifteen minutes of pulling in to Gibson's driveway, Becca and Pam were off to the Dells. The drive was quiet and uneventful as both of the ladies looked forward to the time away from work. There was about an hour of daylight left when Becca pulled the Jeep Cherokee into the campsite, which was located on what had the reputation of being a very good trout stream. It was also located about two miles from the nearest campground and tourist trap. A college friend of Pam's had given her the location and Pam made a mental note to thank him when they got back. Quickly the two ladies unloaded their gear and began to set up camp. The big dome tent, large enough for four, took a little maneuvering to get set up, but in twenty minutes camp was ready and Pam fired up the cook stove to begin making supper.

"So what's for supper, chef?" Becca asked as she took her fly rod from the tubular case and began to assemble it.

"That all depends upon how good you are with that rod," Pam said as she sliced vegetables. "Stir-fry, probably Spam, but hopefully trout if you can snag a couple really quick."

Becca finished tying on a fly and then replied, "I hope I am not too rusty because I hate Spam." With that she headed down to the stream. Tomorrow she would put the waders on and go down river at a leisurely pace; tonight was about not eating Spam, so it was all about catching fish fast. The creek looked like it had a couple of deep spots just above the campsite, so Becca started there. Unhooking the fly from the cork handle, she fed out extra line and then lifted the tip for the first cast of the night. Back and forth she flicked the rod and the fly followed in a graceful arch before landing briefly on the water and then starting its route again as she pulled the rod back. For five minutes, Becca fished, the rustiness of her casts disappearing and the fluidity of her moves returning.

In the stream under a large willow tree, a large branch had fallen into the river during an ice storm in the early winter and the current swirling around it had carved out a deep pool that looked like it could be home to trout. Becca turned her attention to the pool and with the grace of a ballet dancer dropped the fly under the tree. The fly landed softly on the water and just as it was being snatched up into the air the trout's mouth closed over it. Quickly Becca pulled the light rod up into the air, setting the hook firmly in the corner of the large fish's mouth. As the trout felt the hook bite into its mouth, it dove to the bottom pool and then made a run upstream, trying to shake the thing that was biting into its mouth.

The line raced out of the reel as the brook trout fought to shake the hook. When it tired of swimming upstream it turned and swam toward Becca on the downstream leg. Skillfully, Becca played the fish letting it swim away and then pulling in the line as it swam toward her. Each time a little less line was played out and a little more reeled in. Finally the trout tired and Becca deftly scooped it into her fishing net.

Grabbing the fish by the gills she picked up her rod and net and headed back to the camp where Pam would be waiting with the rest of supper.

"Did you catch anything?" Pam called to Becca. "I am famished."

"Only one!" Becca shouted back and held up the large brook trout. "But I think it will do." Once back in camp Becca quickly cleaned and filleted the fish and handed Gibson the filets. Soon Pam was cooking stir-fry on the camp stove, while Becca set about gathering some firewood. Once the fire was started, Becca filled the coffee pot with coffee and water, and then slid it into the coals to perk. The sun was setting and the last of the daylight was fading as they finished dinner and settled around the campfire to relax.

"There is something about the outdoors that is so invigorating," Pam said as she took a long, deep breath. The scent of the breeze as it came off of the river brought back the pleasant memories of her childhood and the camping trips her family had taken. "I am sure glad we were able to get away from the office, even if it was only for a couple of days."

"You know what they say, 'The worst day of fishing is better than the best day of work,'" Becca suggested. "You know about the only thing missing is a couple of hunks to rub oil on us."

"Now that would be a dream come true."

"Wouldn't it though?" They spent the next couple of hours talking and laughing about work, guys, and dreams. Though they had seen each other almost everyday for the last six months, they really hadn't had much time to talk about their lives and goals. In the course of the conversation, Pam mentioned how the Indians used to live and their beliefs in the spirits. This led into a long discussion on Medicine Men and good and evil Spirits.

"I never really believed in that stuff until I started working with you," Pam commented, "but watching you, I think that those beliefs have merit to them."

Becca reached over with the hot mitt and pulled the coffee pot from the fire and poured the dark java into two blue porcelain cups, handing one of the cups to Pam she answered. "As I had studied the tribes, medicine men, and other spiritual leaders, the Indians based their beliefs on reality. I guess the life on the Plains was just too short to believe in something that didn't work."

Sipping the hot coffee, Pam asked, "What do you think about the dream catchers that they sell at the flea markets? Are they real or just a thing to sell?"

"To be honest," Becca began, "I always thought that they weren't much more than pretty trinkets, until last fall just after I got the invitation to speak at the conference. I was feeling a little alone and maybe it was just me feeling sorry for myself, but as I looked at my dream catcher I swear I saw a face in it. When I looked again it was gone. It was really eerie, it felt Jacob Marley-ish and I kept waiting for the ghosts to come, but they never did."

"Wow!" Gibson exclaimed. "Have you seen the face again?"

"Yeah, that is the scary part," Davidson continued, "I see it about once a week, but never at the same time of day. Sometimes morning, other times it appears in the evening. Each time I see the face it becomes a little clearer and the other day I swear the face winked at me."

"Boogie, boogie," Pam laughed, "sounds like bad pizza to me."

"Probably so, but it is interesting to see the face develop in clarity. I hope I meet him someday because the face has a neat twinkle in his eye. Enough talking about my dreams, I am ready to go make some new ones. You can stay up if you want, but I am about beat and am going to get some shut eye." With that she tossed the last of her coffee on the fire and stood to head to the tent.

"Go ahead, I am going to sit up awhile longer," Pam said.

Once Becca got away from the fire, she realized how cool it was. By the time she had slipped out of her clothes and changed into her oversized t-shirt, she had a good shiver going and the flannel of the sleeping bag felt extra soft and warm. As she drifted off to sleep, all she could think of was the twinkle in the eyes and the roguish smile of the face on the wall of her house.

The red morning sun was peaking over the hill when Pam rolled over. Looking at her watch, she couldn't believe that it was morning already. She had opted to stay up after Becca had headed to the tent. First she had tried to call Chris but had only gotten his voicemail, so she had tossed sticks into the fire and watched them burn until her eyes wouldn't stay open any more. Finally when there was only a faint glow of embers, Pam had gone to bed. Running her hands through her hair, Pam looked over at Becca's sleeping bag; she was surprised to find it empty. Quickly she pulled on a fresh t-shirt and a pair of shorts and crawled toward the door of the tent.

"Good morning, sleepy-head!" Becca called out to Pam as she exited the green dome tent. "I thought you were going to sleep all day."

"For Pete's sake, Becca, it is only five thirty in the morning, can't a girl sleep in just once?"

"Not if we are going to catch any trout, you can't. The water is hot, do you want some tea?"

Pam didn't hesitate with her reply, "Oh please, if I have to be awake, then a big mug of tea is what I need and not that decaffeinated stuff. Orange pekoe, long cut please."

Becca had opened up the food stores from the back of the Jeep and dug out the tea bags, the sugar container and some granola bars for breakfast. Neither of the ladies usually ate a big breakfast, so she had chosen the standard fare. Lunch would be a light meal also, but dinner would be worth remembering. They had brought the fixings for a feast and it didn't matter whether the fishing was good or not, they would eat well.

"So are we spincasting or fly-fishing today?" Becca asked Pam between sips of her tea.

"I thought we would fly-fish down the river today and then try out the jigs and spinners tomorrow."

"Fine with me. Barbless hooks?" Davidson replied, referring to the practice of using hooks with barbless tips so that the hook could be removed without excessive damage to the fish's mouth allowing it to be released back into the river.

"Absolutely, that way I can catch the same fish for the next two or three years. Of course I do reserve the right to keep any trophy-size catches."

"Well let's getting going, we're burning daylight," Becca said as she got up and headed to the tent.

"Yeah, it is getting late," Pam said with just a hint of sarcasm in her voice. "What is it? Five fifty? Hurry up!"

When Becca returned from the tent, Pam did a double take to make sure it was her partner. On Becca's head was a multi-colored bucket cap with flies stuck all around it. She wore a khaki fishing vest with all kinds of fishing gadgets in its numerous pockets and loops. It was there that she stopped looking like an ordinary fisherman and more like Becca Davidson, independent woman. A bright purple bikini top was hidden under the vest and a pair of cut off jean shorts that would have made Daisy Duke proud, completed her attire.

"Wow I hope those shorts don't shrink," Pam said as she laughed, knowing full well her outfit would be just as skimpy. With no guys around, neither of the ladies was much on modesty and Pam was actually a little amazed that Becca hadn't appeared in the buff. Quickly Pam ducked into the tent, shucked her t-shirt, and put on her bikini top. Grabbing her fly rod and waders she hustled to catch up with Becca who had already started toward the river. They looked a little strange in shorts and waders, but the stream water was still pretty cold from the spring thaw and if they were going to fly-fish properly it was going to be in the river, not from the bank. Donning their waders they waded out into the cold river, spread out and begin to fish. For the first hour neither made a sound and all that could be heard were a few birds singing and whoosh of the rod and line as it traveled back and forth through the cool morning air.

Pam had the first catch of the morning, landing a medium sized brook trout. After playing the line, she scooped up the fish in her net, carefully removed the hook and set her trout free to swim another day. Within minutes of releasing her catch, Pam heard Becca whoop and begin the fight of landing a rainbow trout. The morning quickly passed as the pair fished their way down stream, catching and releasing various sized brook and rainbow trout. Noon came and Pam called a halt to the fishing for a lunch break. Almost reluctantly they climbed out of the water and up the bank, settling under a large maple tree. Becca and Pam both unshouldered their daypacks and took out the cold lunch that they had brought with them. Granola bars, sliced vegetables, some fruit, and a couple of bottles of flavored water made up their lunch.

"I don't know about you," Becca said as she sliced up an apple. "I am about whipped. I forgot how strenuous it was to walk the river."

"Me too," Pam replied in between sips of water. "I was thinking how good it would be just to nap in the sun this afternoon and work on our tans."

"Oh that does sound great. How far do you think it is back to camp?"

"I think we have fished about a mile downstream," Pam answered. "We should be able to walk along the shore and get back in about a half an hour."

"Let me pull off my waders and we can be on our way back." Becca pulled her hip waders off, rolled them up and put them into a shoulder bag that she had taken from her daypack. Pam had slipped on her hiking sandals and was grabbing her and Becca's rods as Becca cleaned up the bottles and wrappers from lunch.

The hike along the riverbank was easy and they arrived back in camp in twenty-five minutes. They unpacked their waders and fishing gear and set them out to dry. Pam grabbed a couple of beach towels from the tent and laid them out in the sun. Becca rubbed lotion on Pam's back and Gibson returned the favor. As they lay on their stomachs and untied their bikini tops, both had identical thoughts, *this is great and if only I have a man here with me then it would be perfect.*

Becca hummed as she finished getting ready. She had looked forward to today for the last three weeks, ever since Dr. Houchin had told her about the tickets, and she could hardly wait. The opening of the museum exhibit on Native American artifacts was a chance of a lifetime and she was not going to miss it. The place would be packed with historians, archeologists, and other writers, not to mention the philanthropists who financed such exhibits. This was just the place to make the kind of contacts she needed to launch her fledgling teaching and writing careers.

Her bed was covered with a pile of formals and cocktail dresses. Becca had called Rachael and had her bring all her formals over. Each one had been tried on and the discarded as either too revealing or too old maidish. She wanted to look her best, there was no use making a bad impression due to sloppy dress. She finally decided on a long black gown, with a slit to just below mid thigh. A flash of leg, a little cleavage and a man's wallet was easier to open. She chuckled at the thought, her dealings with men had made her a little cynical and she really didn't care who knew.

Smoothing the gown over her hips she turned slowly and looked into the full-length mirror as she did. *Good, no lines*, she thought. She preferred garters and stockings to panty hose because they felt sexier, but she did need to worry about the occasional garter line showing. Not tonight, everything was going perfectly. She piled her red hair up on her head and finished her make up. Sliding on a pair of high-heeled sandals, she headed for the door.

It was a warm June day, but Becca grabbed her wrap anyway. Let the sun go down and she would be shivering to beat the band. Becca left quick note to Rachael, who would probably stop by, on the counter and she was on her way out the door. Becca looked at her watch. If she was lucky, she would miss the evening rush and have plenty of time to get there. If not, she should only be a half-hour late at the most. Not great, but still more than enough time to see the exhibit and meet people. She backed the Jeep Grand Cherokee down the drive into the cul de sac and headed into the city. As she waited at the light to enter the freeway, she turned her radio on and listened to the sounds of a steel guitar playing a country tune. Becca tapped her foot and laughed out loud; she certainly was not dressed to be dancing the Texas Two Step. It didn't matter; she was having a great day.

The trip into the city was uneventful; the interstate was almost empty so Becca pushed the speed limit as far as she dared. The two hours to the museum seemed to fly and before she realized it she was pulling up to the museum. The architects had designed the complex to appeal to both families and intellectuals. The complex was made up of a series of interconnected brick buildings forming an almost star shape complex. A large park with picnic areas surrounded the museum and playgrounds were scattered around. In the southwest corner was a lake, where you could rent a paddleboat by the hour. There were a half a dozen or so boats on the lake and Becca absently wondered what it would be like to be on the lake. The driveway led between the two larger buildings and under a skywalk, on each side there were teepees and wigwams representing every tribe of the Great Plains. At the main entrance, a valet opened the door for her. She handed her keys to him and headed inside, doing her best not to gawk at the building like a tourist.

She checked her wrap and took a glass of champagne from the waiter. Becca was directed down a corridor toward the exhibit area. Sipping on her drink as she walked, Becca looked at each item on display carefully. How she wished that she had brought a notepad or recorder, as many of the items would be useful in her next article. The museum was becoming crowded as more and more people arrived.

# Chapter 8

Roy sat on the edge of his bed and stared into the closet. He didn't want to go and except for the fact that his firm had helped finance the expedition, he would not have gone. That was probably the biggest drawback of being a partner in the firm. While all the managers could beg off at these boring events, the partners were expected to be there. It had been a risky venture to finance an archeological expedition into the Badlands to search for Native American artifacts. The expedition had been extremely successful and had found a Sioux tribe winter camp dating back into the 1400s. The artifacts found would provide great insight into how the Plains people lived.

Reluctantly he stood and removed one of the tuxedos from the closet. The tux was western cut, with a long frock coat and bright red vest. Paul would probably give him the evil eye and a lecture about dignified dress, but if he had to go he was dressing the way he wanted to. Roy ran a polishing rag across his black stingray skin boots and then pulled them on. He had stalled as long as he dared. Grabbing his black Stetson off the hat rack he headed out the door.

The elevator door opened to the parking garage and the warm late spring air hit Roy in the face. By the time he reached his parking space, Curtis knew that it was a "BMW convertible with the top down" kind of evening. The top went down quickly and Roy hopped in without opening the door and started the sports car up. Hooking his hat into the holder behind the seat, Curtis backed out of the space and headed out of the garage. He waved to the doorman as he exited onto the street, a little faster than was necessary, but not enough to squeal the tires. Roy enjoyed maneuvering the BMW through traffic, so soon he was weaving in and out like a slalom skier.

The CD player was playing a Brooks & Dun tune full blast as he cruised down the freeway. Roy was thoroughly enjoying the drive and just about missed the turn off. He saw it at the last second; fortunately he was in the right lane and whipped the car onto the exit ramp just before the crash barrels. Pulling up to the entrance, he hopped over the side of the car, tossed the keys to the valet, put on his Stetson and headed for the door.

"Your invitation please." The doorman put his hand in front of Curtis, stopping him.

"Invitation?" Roy looked at him with a puzzled look. Then the light came on. Helen had laid an invitation on his desk this afternoon and he had promptly walked off and forgotten it. "I am sorry. I seem to have left it at the office, my name is on the list, Roy R. Curtis. I am with Lescowitch, Meier, Curtis and Sheridan Investment Bankers."

"If you will wait here, I will check," the doorman said, obviously not believing this cowboy. He shut the door and spoke into a radio. A second later the doorman mumbled, *"Very good,"* into the mic.

"I am sorry for the delay, sir," still not believing, but following orders. "Your invitation has been verified and you may proceed. Please have a good evening."

"Thank you, Fritz," Curtis said sarcastically as he entered the museum. He could tell he was going to love this evening. *Such fun, hooray, hooray. Maybe I will get plastered on cheap champagne and get hauled off to jail.* Well it was a thought not too likely to happen but a thought nonetheless. He checked his hat and headed to look for a place to hide. When Jacki had been alive he had enjoyed such events but not anymore. *Just stay put and out of trouble, Curtis.*

As he walked through the exhibit area, he looked at the artifacts. They had mixed in drawings and paintings of the Sioux tribe so it wasn't too boring. He sipped a glass of bubbly as he looked at a picture of Sitting Bull. It was hard to believe that he had led the battle at the Little Big Horn, but he had.

"Well, Mr. Curtis, you're looking nice this evening." The sweet voice and strong perfume startled him and he jumped. That resulted in a giggle from the lady who was already working on one too many glasses of champagne.

"Oh, hi, Tonya. You are looking nice also," Roy said politely. Tonya Robertson was a newspaper reporter slash golddigger, who had her sights set on Roy Curtis. She always seemed to show up at functions like these. Not that she wasn't good looking, dressed in a slinky black cocktail dress that showed all the curves; it was just that she had one thing on her mind, getting Roy Curtis in the sack. Curtis hated pushy women and Tonya was among the pushiest.

"So how is my cowboy?" Tonya took his arm like they were lovers and pulled herself close. Curtis wanted to pull away and scream at her but better judgment took over for the second time this evening.

"Fine, thank you," he answered coldly. Roy thought he would try the cold shoulder approach instead. He knew it wouldn't work, but he would try it anyway. She was beautiful and her perfume was intoxicating; part of him wanted to find a back room and taste of her wares, but in the long run he figured carnal lust with this woman would be way too expensive. The problem now was how to disengage without being rude or causing a scene. He looked around the room for a quick solution but none was forthcoming.

Becca was taking her time going through the exhibition hall, absorbing the detail of each piece and committing it to memory. She mentally beat herself again for not bringing at least a recorder to take notes with. Hopefully she could still remember everything by the time she got back home and to her laptop. As Becca reached the center of the museum, she decided to get a bite to eat at the buffet that had been set up. Turning the corner, an artifact caught her eye and she absentmindedly headed to look at it first.

"Oh, excuse me." Becca had walked right into the side of a gentleman.

"No pardon needed." As the man straightened his jacket, Becca noticed he was a small man, probably in his sixties, with silver hair. His face showed evidence of many hours in the sun and wind. The wrinkles resembled the hills and valleys of the terrain he had spent years working in. "My name in Sam Markus, and whom do I have the pleasure of meeting?"

"Rebecca Davidson. You can call me Becca, though." Becca smiled at the elderly gentleman.

"I was just heading over to the buffet when you bumped into me. Would you care to join me?" The wrinkles on his face came alive as he smiled. "And call me Sam. Are you an archeologist? I thought I knew most everyone in my field."

"Hardly, I am a writer and a history buff, amateur at the best."

"So how did a lovely lady like you get into this exclusive showing?"

The hair on the back of her neck stood straight out with that comment. This man, as nice as he may appear, was as condescending as most of the others she had met. She decided to give him the light response rather than the left hook like she wanted.

"Really, I am a mechanic and I fixed the semi that brought the stuff so they gave me a ticket." Becca giggled like an air- headed blonde. Markus took the bait and laughed too, a whole lot louder than was needed. Taking Becca's arm he led her to the buffet table. As they walked, Markus took another glass of champagne and gulped it down. She wondered how many of those he had already. When they got in line, Markus let her go first. As she passed by him, Becca felt his hand brush her thigh. Taking a deep breath and rolling her eyes back, she hoped that it was accidental and not intentional, because she really didn't want to make a scene.

The food looked delicious and it tasted every bit as good as it looked. She tried to engage Sam in some meaningful conversation as they walked the line but it soon became obvious to her that her breasts were more important to him than her thoughts on Native

American culture. The short man stared straight into her cleavage as he talked about his adventures as an archeologist. As Becca tried unsuccessfully several times to part company with him, each time he managed to block her exit. On and on he droned, moving closer and closer to her as he talked until she could feel his breath on her chest. Slowly and steadily a crowd gathered around the two, partly because they were near the end of the buffet line and partly because Markus was famous.

Encouraged by the crowd and the champagne, Markus continued to regale his tales to the crowd. Becca was beginning to think, from the way this little man boasted; that he was Indiana Jones incarnate. Davidson wanted so badly to leave, but all she could do was smile and stand there. Here she was being breathed on by a pompous drunk, when the whole museum was full of artifacts worth looking at. Desperately she looked around the crowd for a familiar face from the university, but none was to be found. Sullenly, she resigned herself to being confined by the crowd.

Since Roy couldn't figure any quick way to disengage the golddigger from his arm, he figured he would bore her to death. *At least I will have company then when I die of boredom*, he thought. Ever so slowly he began his way around the exhibit, looking closely at each piece and reading all the information as he came to it. About five minutes through the back of the exhibit, Roy realized that he was actually enjoying himself. It had been so long since he had absorbed information, just for the sake of learning. He was surprised to find out how relaxing it was. Tonya, on the other hand, was not having a good time at all. She kept pulling on his arm trying to speed him up, but Roy was moving at a snail's pace and was not going to move any faster.

"Good evening, Roy," Paul Lescowitch greeted his partner. Paul enjoyed these types of events just for the sake of the event. He took pleasure in wearing his tux and parading his beautiful wife, Ann of twenty-five years around for all to see. Tonight was no exception; Ann looked as beautiful as ever in her formal, a single strand of pearls encircling her neck. The way the Lescowitchs dressed and walked seem to scream "look at me I'm rich", in a very elegant way. Old money always seemed to emit that kind of feeling and the Lescowitch's money was as old as any.

"Good evening, sir. Ma'am," Roy always called him sir out of habit and respect. Even though they were equal partners in the firm, Roy always felt that Mr. Lescowitch always deserved his respect and his Marine Corps training would not let him do otherwise. "You look elegant as always Ann. I believe you know Miss Robertson."

"Yes, I do," Paul, said with a smile. Tonya had been chasing Roy for over two years, never catching, just chasing. "You look very nice tonight. Do try to act like a gentleman tonight, Roy, and not the cowboy you're dressed as."

*Here it comes, digs and reprimands, just because I don't ooze with old money.*

"Paul, leave him alone," Ann scolded her husband. "I know that he is not a stuffed shirt like you, but he is the best at what he does. Besides I think he looks fine, real fine." Ann winked at Roy. Roy could never figure out if she was just playing or really trying to get Roy to make a move on her. Curtis just laughed because he knew it would never happen.

"OK, sorry, Roy, it's just that...."

"I know, sir, our money and reputation are on the line. I promise to be good and not pull out my six-shooter and wreak revenge for the Little Big Horn."

"What worries me is that someday you just might pull that gun. Oh, by the way, have you seen Sheridan? If you do, tell him to look me up, I need to talk to him before morning. Come along, Ann, I am famished." With that, Paul led Ann away toward the buffet, once again leaving Curtis alone with Tonya.

"Have a good evening, sir. Thanks for leaving me," Curtis muttered.

"What did you say, cowboy? Tonya asked.

"Nothing, Tonya, nothing. Let's look at some more artifacts."

"OK, maybe later you could show me some of your etchings?" Tonya pressed her breasts tight against him. All Roy could do was roll his eyes heavenward and pray he could find a way to ditch her and soon. Being slow and thoughtful hadn't worked, maybe food would untangle this bimbo, albeit a smart bimbo, but still a bimbo, from around his arm. Without rushing, but not delaying either, Roy made his way back to the main room, bimbo in tow.

The line to the buffet was long so there was no immediate relief from Tonya's perfume. Standing in line, Roy gave her another glass of champagne. Curtis scanned the room once again for help. If Mike was here he might be able to pawn her off on him. Mike was the playboy of the partners and wouldn't mind the company of a good-looking woman. He spotted Ann and Paul standing in the corner talking to another couple. Roy recognized Mike's football player physique, but didn't know the lady on his arm. Even with her back to him he could tell that she was a looker. So much for pawning Tonya off on Sheridan.

Tonya was babbling on about something to do with her career and how she was being held back. "You know they just don't appreciate me for my mind. If they would give me a meaningful assignment instead of these stupid exhibits...."

Roy did his best to tune her out, but she just droned on. She never even slowed down when he handed her a plate. He tried to distance himself from her by going down the opposite side of the buffet, but she backed out of the line she was in and broke into his line. *Good grief! What a leech! Is this woman ever going to go away?*

They were almost at the end of the buffet when he noticed a crowd of men just off to his right. Roy thought maybe he could do a three card Monty and lose Tonya before she figured out what was going on. He turned to move through the crowd toward them, when he saw a lady standing in the middle of the men. From the way she was looking around it was obvious to Roy that she was trying to find way to escape from the group. Tall and beautiful, her red hair was piled high on her head. She looked his way and though he had always thought it a little silly in the movies, their gaze met and locked. Stopping in his tracks, he stood there transfixed on this beacon of red hair as her sapphire blue eyes pierced straight to his heart. Roy shook his head and regained his senses; his sudden stop had caused Tonya to stumble and spill part of her plate. He ignored her as she tried to find a napkin to wipe the fruit salad off her dress and walked straight toward the group. Robertson, tipsy from the champagne, cursed at him but he just kept walking.

Pushing his big bull frame against the others, he made his way through the crowd. When he reached the center where she was standing he could see the little man pressing against her. Looking at her, he extended his hand toward her. She looked at his hand and then as if they were old friends, clasped it between both of her own.

"I have been looking all over for you," Roy greeted her as he inserted himself between her and Markus.

"I have been standing here waiting," she replied. "Now that you have found me, may we go?"

"Certainly, this way if you please." Roy turned and led the way out. He said, "Excuse me," as he headed out, but it was more like, "Gangway!" or "Make a hole!" or any of the other terms he used in the Marines when he needed to get through a crowd. He led her out of the gallery and to the front door. The doorman jumped up to summon his car, but Roy just waved him off and turned towards the plaza. The plaza between the buildings and lake was a beautifully landscaped botanical area featuring plants native to the region.

"You saved me from a fate worse than death. Thank you," she said as sat down on one of the park benches. "I wasn't sure how long I was going to last. What prompted you to come barging in like the cavalry to the rescue? Not that I'm complaining, just curious."

"Purely personal reasons," was his reply, then a large smile crossed his face. "I saw it as a chance to make a getaway with a lovely lady and to dump the golddigger that had latched onto me."

"Well, thank you again, I think. Since you have me out here, do you mind if I sit here for a couple of minutes? My feet are killing me. That little professor had me leaning on my heels for close to a half an hour."

"May I join you then?"

"Most certainly."

"I guess I should properly introduce myself. My name is Roy Curtis," Roy offered his hand.

Taking his hand, she replied, "My name is Rebecca Davidson, but my rescuers get the privilege of calling me Becca."

"OK, Becca, what's a nice girl like you doing in a place like this?"

Becca laughed at the cliché and tossed one right back at him, "Why looking for my cowboy to take me off into the sunset."

"Touché."

"Actually, I am a part time writer and a lecturer at Moluntha State over in the Quad Cities. And you?"

"Investment banker doing his duty by keeping the clients happy." The wrought iron bench was about eight-feet long, so he turned and leaned back into the corner and looked at Becca. There was something about her that said she was more than a writer, but he couldn't put his finger on it at the moment.

Taking her cue from Roy, she tucked her legs underneath her and turned in her seat. "An investment banker, hmmm, I would have placed you on the back of a horse with a rope in your hand."

"My other occupation," Roy admitted, "I also own a fair-sized farm in northern Indiana. So I get to spend weekends at the farm. And you?"

"School bus mechanic," she said matter-of-factly.

"Really?" Roy said with genuine interest, not the condescending way that Markus had said just a little while before. "Do you work for a school or a private company?"

"A small school about two hours east of here, I was the head bus driver and mechanic until I joined the staff at Moluntha State. Now I am a consultant per se, it lets me turn a wrench now and then."

"I'm impressed. So how did you end up here being bored to death?" For the next fifteen minutes the two exchanged brief versions of their stories. Becca told him about her job with the university and Roy told her about life in Chicago as a partner in an investment-banking firm. Both skillfully kept their guards up, saying a lot but telling each other nothing. Finally Roy stood up and took Becca by the hand and helped her up. Side by side they walked through the garden area, the fragrance of the late spring blooms filling the air. Taking their time, the pair meandered through the botanical display pointing to the various plants and stopping occasionally to read a placard about some bush or pretty tree neither noticing that they were walking a little closer or that the tone of their voices had changed.

The path ended at the beach, the sun was halfway over the horizon and the sky shone brightly in hues of red and orange. Becca stopped at the sand's edge and looked out over the water. A gentle warm spring breeze sent ripples of water across the surface. The beauty of the evening landscape penetrated deep into her heart. A sudden urge hit Becca. She knew what she wanted to do, she wanted to run like a school child over the sand and let the edge of water play tag with her toes. The feeling was a familiar one, but one that she had long forgotten. Becca lifted her left foot to remove her sandal, but stumbled as her right heel sank into the sand.

"I've got you." Becca felt his hands catch her.

"Thanks," Becca flushed slightly as he held her, "the sand is a little softer than I thought." His hands felt nice against her side and she made no attempt to stand up. Reaching down, Becca slipped off her shoes one at a time, then she pulled the hem of her dress up so that she could unfasten her stockings. It was Roy's turn to blush as he caught himself staring at her long, stockinged legs. Shyly he averted his gaze, wondering why he was embarrassed. Her sandals and stockings off, Becca stood back up and ran down the beach. She ran backwards and motioned Roy to follow.

Curtis wasn't the spur of the moment type of guy, so he hesitated slightly when the she waved at him. It was only an instant that he delayed, but it was long enough that Becca's countenance changed. He just shook his head and smiled and headed after her. When Roy got within arm's reach, she giggled and ran off. Like two children playing tag they chased each other, touching briefly and then parting. Both were breathless from the game when Becca lifted her gown up to her knees and ran out fifteen feet into the water. Roy stood on the edge of the water with his hands on his hips and looked at her.

Teasingly she taunted him and made faces at him. Roy started to take his boots off and then stopped. He motioned with his finger for her to join him on shore and when she didn't, he walked out to her, boots, tux and all. In one quick motion, he lifted her out of the water and carried her back to shore.

Gently he set her down on the shore until her toes sunk into the sand. Becca stood looking at him in amazement; never had a man done something like that with her. Here this man had waded knee deep in water without caring whether or not he ruined a tux and a pair of boots. Unconsciously she took his hand and they started to walk back up the sand. Becca picked up her sandals and stockings and they continued around the edge of the beach. The sun was behind the hills and the breeze had turned cool, so Roy stopped and put his long coat over her shoulders. Leaving his arm around her, he pulled her close and headed for the dock. Together they sat on a bench on the dock, this time not at opposite ends, but with Becca leaning on Roy's shoulder.

Both sat silently, leaning on each other, but their minds raced with a collection of emotions and thoughts. *Was it possible,* Roy thought, *that after all these years someone so beautiful could enter into my life?* Not since the wreck so many years before had he felt the passion in his soul. Becca wondered if this man could be as genuine as he seemed or if the hypocrisy would creep out after a couple of dates.

Breaking the trance, Curtis leaned forward and pulled off his soggy boots. Water streamed out of the boot as he turned it upside down. Becca giggled as the water splattered against the wood of the dock.

"What?" Roy asked, looking at her.

"It's just that…," Becca giggled harder, "you looked so…," Becca was laughing so hard now the she held her sides and stomped her feet in laugher, "gallant…in the water. And now so…silly." The words came in short spurts in between gasps for air and laughter.

Incredulously Roy looked at her and then he started to laugh. Soon he was laughing as hard as she was. When they finally calmed down, they could hear the first of the crowd from the exhibition starting to leave. Reluctantly, and with great difficulty, Roy pulled his boots back on. The wet stingray skin squeaked in protest as he pulled hard on the loops. The squish of his wet socks caused Becca to giggle once again, but she put her hand over mouth when Roy looked at her. Hand in hand they walked back to the museum. Becca offered to get his hat and her wrap so he wouldn't have to go in, but Roy insisted. Walking into the hall like he didn't have a care in the world, no coat and boots squishing, Roy collected his hat and Becca's wrap. Stopping by the valet's desk he collected their keys, tipping the valet and telling him they would walk to the parking lot and yes, he knew it was a long ways out there. Fortunately he didn't run into Tonya or Paul and Ann and made it back out to where Becca was standing.

It was about a quarter of a mile out to the parking lot and normally either of them could have easily walked it in five minutes, but it took closer to ten. Neither wanted the evening to end, they had both laughed more they had in years. Becca looked at Roy and asked, "I wonder if your golddigger and my roaming hand archeologist had as much fun as we did?"

"Somehow I doubt it, Ms. Davidson, somehow I greatly doubt it," he said with a chuckle.

The sky was crystal clear and the moon shone brightly across the parking lot. They had arrived to the exhibition at just about the same time so their cars were parked fairly close together. Stopping at her Jeep, Roy unlocked the door and handed her the keys. It was decision time for both of them, do they end this evening and go their separate ways or continue the night together and maybe regret it in the morning? Taking his coat from her shoulders, he put her wrap around her. Taking her hands in his, Roy stood looking at Becca.

"What are you thinking, Mr. Curtis?" Becca asked with more than a little trepidation.

"I was thinking of how fine you look in the moonlight and how this has been the most enjoyable evening I have had in a very long time and how I am carrying on like a school boy." Roy smiled. "Would you mind if I were to call you next week?"

Becca looked into his face, returned his smile and answered, "I would love for you to call." Fishing around in her purse she pulled out a business card and handed it to him. "Here, this has my office and my cell phone numbers on it."

"Thank you and I promise I will." Roy handed her one of his cards. His hands were still holding hers and he leaned forward and lightly kissed her on the cheek. The softness of the red lips tempted him to take a second kiss, but he stopped because the last thing he wanted to do was offend her now.

"Thank you for the best evening I have had in years," he said as Becca slid behind the wheel.

"You are most welcome and thank you." Roy shut her door and watched as she drove off. Becca waved to him as she pulled out. Roy walked over to his BMW and leaned against the hood. How long he leaned there he wasn't sure, all he knew was that his life had change tonight and changed for the better.

Becca looked in the Jeep's mirror as she pulled out of the museum driveway. She felt like it had been a dream. Becca still felt dream-like when she pulled into her own drive. Rachael's car was still parked at the curb; Becca could hardly wait to tell her about the evening. She hit the garage door like a debutant home from the prom. Hit was probably the wrong word, floated was a better description.

"Hey, Rach!" Becca hollered as she entered the kitchen, the TV clicked off and Rachael came in from the living room.

"So, how did it go?" Rachael asked as she opened the refrigerator and pulled out a couple of Diet Pepsis.

"It was great, you have seen the artifacts, I hope I can remember everything I saw and read." Becca started in describing all about the evening including Sam Markus' trapping her in the corner.

Rach interrupted her, "So how did you get away?"

"You're not going to believe this, but a cowboy came to the rescue." That led to the telling of the rest of the evening with Roy Curtis.

"You really waded out in the pond?"

"Yep."

"And he actually walked in and carried you out?"

"Wow, I hope you got his phone number."

"I did and he has mine. He also asked if he could call."

Rachael asked, "Do you think he will or was he blowing smoke?"

Becca smiled and replied, "If he was blowing smoke, it was the best smoke that has been blown my way in a long time." Then with a slight sigh added, "Oh I sure hope he calls."

# Chapter 9

Roy awoke thirty minutes before the alarm clock was scheduled to make like a bad imitation of a rooster and greet the day. He had gotten home about two in the morning and it was now five-thirty, only three and a half hours and yet he felt more refreshed that he had in years. The early morning sun was casting its beam through the window of the Little Italy apartment and onto the Queen Anne chair in the corner. Sitting up he spied the dirty tuxedo and shirt lying crumpled up on the chair. In two steps he was over to the tux, picked up the trousers. Reaching into the pocket he pulled out a business card and read it. Roy held the card close to his face and inhaled, ever so slightly he could smell her fragrance. The card and fragrance verified that last night had been real and not a dream. Carefully he slipped the card into his wallet and headed to the bathroom.

His wet boots were on the floor by the bathroom door. He laughed as he picked up the soggy stingray skin boots. If he had been drunk he could have written this off to hard liquor. He must have been crazy to walk into the water wearing eight hundred dollar handmade boots. Fortunately they would dry and they would be good as new. He turned on the boot drying rack and placed the boots upside down over the air tubes. The tubes circulated air inside the boots so that the leather would dry and not crack.

Satisfied that the boots would dry and not be ruined, Roy proceeded with his morning ritual of getting ready for work. After a quick shave and shower he walked over to the closet. Looking at his suits, for some reason unknown to him, each one of the suits looked a little stuffy, kind of drab and just plain boring. He had never really thought about what he wore to work, the only thing that wasn't traditional bankers garb were his boots. He had worn western boots since he was a little shaver and rode around the farm on a Shetland pony. His closet contained about fifteen different pairs, from his old wing tips he had worn in college to the stingray skins that were drying on the rack. Even the oldest pair were shined and well taken care of, the soles having been replaced many times and the tops slouching with age. Jacki had teased him of spending more time caring for his boots than he cared for her. Well, it was a banker boring day, a dark gray suit, white shirt and a red tie. Pulling the knot into place, Roy was dressed and ready to go just as the alarm clock crowed. Roy shut the alarm off and headed out of the apartment and into the garage. It was going to be a warm muggy day in Chicago, so the rag top on the Z4 came down and with the morning breeze in his face, he zipped off to work.

The traffic was surprisingly light and Roy made a mental note to try to go to work early every morning. Roosevelt Ave. was usually very slow going during rush hour, but the BMW rolled along at about thirty-five miles per hour. Michigan Ave. traffic was just as sparse as it had been on Roosevelt. What was usually an hour of stop-and-go turned into a pleasant thirty-minute drive. It was just six forty-five when Curtis eased his sports car into his reserved parking spot in the Van Buren Street parking garage. The garage was about two blocks from the office and was connected to the adjoining buildings via skywalks. It was entirely possible to walk from his parking spot to his desk without going out in the weather. It was a feature that he utilized frequently, but today, he felt like walking in the sunshine.

The small café located just around the corner from the office building opened every morning at six, but most of the time Roy Curtis was in just too big of a hurry to notice or to care. Today the aroma of the fresh coffee and bagels seduced him and he found himself sitting down for a French toast bagel with melted butter and a cup of Earl Gray tea. Sitting at a table on the patio, Roy watched the people rush by. He wondered how many times he had done just the same, oblivious to this little shop and the quietness it contained. Finished with his meal, he paid the bill and left a tip, which was larger than normal, and headed to the office.

The teapot whistled its tune, signaling that the water was hot. Becca mimicked the notes back as she walked into the kitchen. It was almost eight o'clock, but Becca didn't care. No seminars were scheduled and Becca had told Pam not to worry about showing up until ten that morning. She had figured that she would be out late and could use the extra rest. What a night. Who would have thought that at an archeological exhibition she would have met her cowboy? Becca smiled and laughed at the thought and continued making her breakfast. Glancing over at the dream catcher, Becca thought she recognized the face in the middle, but it quickly faded.

Gibson's bright red Pontiac was in its parking spot when Becca pulled in. Pam was never one to be late even on days she was allowed to be. She always had things to do and presentations to perfect. More than once Becca had to shoo her out of the office on Friday night, reminding her assistant that there was a life on the outside.

Pam handed Ms. Davidson a cup of Earl Gray tea as she sat down at her desk. No sooner had Becca settled into her chair and taken a sip of the tea, than Pam asked the question.

"Well, how was it?"

"It was wonderful." Becca propped her feet up on the corner of her desk and thought of the evening. "The air was perfect, the moonlight glistened off the lake, and we walked…."

"Whoa there, trot that by me again," Pam interrupted. "I asked you about the exhibition and you are sounding as if you had a romantic date."

"Never mind, just dreaming. The exhibition was great. You should have seen the artifacts, some of them make our stuff look like dime store imitations. They had it laid out exquisitely; you could walk through a complete history of the tribe." Davidson babbled on for the next several minutes about the historical significance of the find and how it would help them teach kids better. Suddenly and ever so slightly her thoughts shifted back to that cowboy. "I met this archeologist, who probably had spent too much time in the sun and at least six months without looking at a beautiful woman. Anyway he cornered me and I thought I was going to have to defend my honor when he came and rescued me and then we walked...."

"Stop the train. That's twice now you have mentioned we and he and walking in connection with last night and don't tell me nothing because that dog won't hunt. Understand?"

"I understand," Becca agreed, "but I am not sure exactly how it happened, so I will stick to what I do know. Anyway as I was saying, I was cornered by this scientist and several of his colleagues who were trying to make an archeological find inside my dress. I was this far from slapping him when this cowboy came barreling in like the Lone Ranger, took my hand like we were old friends and led me out of the room."

"You're kidding me, Becca."

"Honest, Pam, that's what happened. This cowboy was decked out in a tux that would have made any of the old west gamblers proud. I mean long coat, vest, and the works."

"Pretty ostentatious, wasn't it? Dressing up like a cowboy at an Indian affair."

"Probably right, but somehow I don't think it was ego as much as it was style because he acted like the genuine thing."

"Anyway back to your story, this cowboy comes busting in and takes you away?"

"Yeah, just like we had been friends for years and since I was looking for an escape route, I followed his lead. It turns out we were both looking for a way out, so we left the museum and walked through the gardens and then talked a while. He was so real and reserved I almost thought it was an act, so I was a little reserved. I didn't want him to think I was too eager. After we sat on a bench and talked, we watched the sun go down over the pond and then he walked me to my car and we said good night and that's the end of the story." Becca said leaving the part about the water and him carrying her to shore.

"Somehow I don't think it is the whole story. Does this cowboy have a name? Is he good looking? Did you get his phone number? Do you think he will call? Do you want him to call?" Gibson fired the questions off so fast that Becca didn't have time to answer. When Pam took a breath, Becca started to respond.

"Yes, he does have a name: Roy Curtis. He is a partner in an investment banking firm. Good looking, yeah, in a rugged sort of a way. Reminds you of a cowboy I guess. Broad shoulders, blue eyes, big mustache and a smile a mile wide when he laughs." Davidson reached in her purse and pulled out his card. She placed it carefully, as if it was made of fragile crystal, on the front of her Rolodex, a business card with a phone number. "He asked if he could call next week and oh how I pray he does." She leaned back and stared at the ceiling, the images of him wading out into the water and picking her up danced in front of her mind.

At exactly seven forty-five, Roy Curtis walked into the office. The office manager, Helen Peterson, was at her usual position at the front desk. She had her own office, where she directed the administrative affairs of the firm, but she always sat at the front desk from seven to eight in the morning to handle the telephone and crises of the moment. The rest of the office staff arrived at eight, but Helen opened the firm every morning at seven, made coffee and sorted the stack of newspapers for the partners. Paul preferred the *New York Times*. John read the *Tribune* and *The Wall Street Journal*. *USA Today's* sports section made the top of Sheridan's pile followed by *Barron's*. Roy perused *The Wall Street Journal* plus a couple of trade newsletters that were faxed or emailed every day. Helen handed him the papers and a stack of phone messages that had accumulated since he left yesterday afternoon.

"You're looking cheerful this morning," Ms. Peterson commented. "How was the opening last night? Did you enjoy yourself?'

"Yeah, it was all right." Roy's mind flashed back to Becca standing in the water. He stood there for a second relishing the memory before he answered. "Come to think of it, last night was a great evening." With that he headed down to his office lost in thought. He nearly bumped into Paul as he meandered down the hall.

"What's up with Roy?" Helen asked the firm's senior partner. "You would almost think he was in love. Did something happen last night that I should know about?"

"Not that I know of, the last time that Ann or I saw him he was doing his best to ditch Tonya Robertson."

"The reporter?"

"The same. She had a death grip on his arm and wasn't letting go." Lescowitch answered as he took sip of his morning coffee.

"Roy can't stand her," Ms. Peterson said. "How did she ever get close to him?"

"I am not sure, but she was doing a great imitation of a leech."

Mike Sheridan and John Meier II walked in the door and caught most of the short conversation. Mike offered his version of last night. "I saw what happened last night. Somebody bumped that Robertson gal in the buffet line and spilled food on her. When she stopped to wipe her dress, Curtis did a beeline for the tall redhead that was in the middle of this group of men and like old friends, they walked out the door."

"Well that explains what I saw as I left last night," John joined in. "As I was leaving, in the other door comes Curtis, no coat, his boots and pants soaking wet. I might have said something if the gala had not all ready been over. Anyway as I walked out the door there is this gorgeous redhead standing in a corner wearing what appeared to be Roy's long coat around her shoulders."

"You don't think Curtis actually found someone do you?" Paul questioned.

"If he did, she must be pretty special," Helen decreed. "So let's be the wise people that we pretend to be and leave him alone." That ended the conversation and each of the partners headed to his respective office. Ms. Peterson had spoken in the matter of office gossip and it was law.

The morning passed without any more talk of the previous night. Roy settled into his daily routine of meetings and telephone calls. Curtis was working on about a half a dozen projects all in various stages of completion. Staff members hustled in and out of the partners' offices with questions and progress reports. About eleven the intercom rang, Curtis punched the speaker button and spoke.

"Yeah, Nicole."

"Sir, there is a Ms. Tonya Robertson on the telephone. I tried to take a message but she insisted on talking to you. She said she knows you are there because your BMW is in the garage. I can tell her you are in a meeting."

Curtis looked at his watch, "That's OK, Nicole, I will take it. Putting her off would only postpone the inevitable."

"Line six then, sir." With that the intercom went dead. Roy reached over and with a big sigh, picked up the receiver and lit up line six.

"Roy Curtis speaking."

"You weren't very nice last night," the voice on the phone said.

"I don't know what you mean," Roy said, playing a little dumb.

"Don't get coy with me, Roy Curtis. You know exactly what I mean, leaving me in the buffet line with a mess on my dress and wandering off with that Amazon woman."

For some reason that statement pulled Roy's chain and he snapped back at her with viciousness in his voice. "Listen here, you floozy! If I had wanted to stay with a golddigger like you, I would have chosen someone with a lot more class and whose hair and eyebrows were the same color!"

"Fine. I don't care if I never see you again!"

"Fine with me!" With that Roy slammed down the phone. He looked up and Helen was standing in the door. She looked at him quizzically.

"Is everything OK?" Having heard about his run in with the reporter, she wondered how that was going to play out with the rumored mystery woman.

"Everything is fine," Roy answered and then he thought for a moment. "Yes, everything is fine." A smile crossed his face as Becca's face crossed his mind. The smile widened and he looked up at Helen and spoke. "Excuse me, Helen, I think I need to make a call."

"No problem." Helen smiled and backed out the door, closing it as she left. As soon as the door was closed, Roy reached into his pocket for his wallet and found the card he carefully placed there earlier that morning. Dialing the number that was printed in the corner, he waited as the phones connected and began to ring. Each ring made him jump. He was as nervous as he had been when he was a college boy and was calling a coed for that first date. Part of him prayed with each ring no one was there. The other part longed for her to answer so that he could hear her voice again.

"History Department, this is Sharon, how may I direct your call?" The strange voice startled Roy and for a second he just about hung up.

"Umm, Ms. Davidson, please."

"May I tell her who is calling?" the receptionist inquired.

"Roy Curtis. I am with Lescowitch, Meier, Curtis, & Sheridan," Roy stated, trying to sound confident.

"Just a second." He was put on hold and the musack started to play.

Sharon shook her head as she dialed the office that Ms. Davidson shared with her assistant wondering when the brokers would figure out that university employees didn't have any money and that everyone would be better served if they would not bother calling. The phone rang twice before Pam Gibson picked up the phone.

"Native American Seminars, Pam speaking." The two of them never answered the phone the same way so Sharon was never sure how to respond.

"Pam, Ms. Davidson has a call on line two. A Roy Curtis from some important sounding firm, Mouscowitch and Oscar Meyer, I think, probably a salesperson. Shall I take a message?"

"Just a second, I'll check." Pam covered the receiver with her hand and looked over at Becca. "It's Roy Curtis, shall she take a message?"

"Give me the phone." Becca reached over and grabbed at the phone. Pam kept it out of her reach and told Sharon to send the call through. Teasingly she finally handed it to Becca. Becca took a deep breath and answered as professionally as she could.

"This is Ms. Davidson. How may I help you?"

"Hello. This is Roy Curtis from the exhibition last night. I know I asked if I could call you next week, but I was wondering if you were free for dinner tonight and if you were, would you care to join me?" Roy's heart was pounding as he asked. The fear of rejection caused him to shake and sweat.

"Let me check my schedule." Becca cupped her had over the receiver and whispered to Pam. "He's asking me to supper tonight. What should I do?"

"Go, silly girl," Pam whispered back.

Taking her hand off the receiver, she said, "I have a meeting at five but I could be ready about six-thirty."

"Six-thirty will be fine. Where shall I pick you up?"

"How about my place? It's just off I-80 near Peru."

"Sounds great, what's the address?" Becca gave him her home address. Roy confirmed it and then said good bye. Leaning back in the chair, Becca smiled.

"It's going to be a great day, Pam. Let's get some work done." With those words she picked up a stack of notes and started to sort through them.

# Chapter 10

Becca wasn't the only one smiling after the phone call, Roy felt almost giddy with delight. He sat there staring at the telephone not believing that he actually had a date that he was looking forward to going on. He thought for a second and then picked up the telephone and dialed Mrs. Peterson's extension.

"Mrs. Peterson, can you do me a favor?" Roy always used her surname when he needed a personal favor and it had gotten to be a standard among the partners.

"Certainly, what do you need, Mr. Curtis?"

"Mrs. Peterson, please call Vinnie to make reservations and tell him private and important."

"Very good, sir. Private and important. Should I have flowers delivered?"

"What do I need flowers for?" Roy was suddenly embarrassed that he had been found out. "Thank you, Mrs. Peterson. You are very thoughtful. One red rose, I do believe, will be sufficient for tonight. Oh and have the limousine out front around eight forty-five."

"Consider it done." The intercom was silent.

The rest of the afternoon crept by, finally four thirty came around and Curtis was out the door. He was nervous and it showed as he banged the wheel of the BMW. The slow traffic leaving downtown seemed to heighten his nervousness and when he finally hit the open freeway, he floored the German sports car as if it were on the Autobahn. Greased lightning would have had a hard time keeping up with the dark blue BMW. Thoughts ran through his mind as fast as the car was heading down the interstate. Was she really as pretty as he remembered? Would the magic of last night still be there? He turned off of the freeway with just ten minutes to find her house. Roy looked at the directions he had written down. The address was 315 Briarwood. Go to the second light turn right, through two stop signs turn left at the Dairy King, then turn right on to Briarwood. Slowly Roy counted down the houses. Three oh nine, three eleven, three thirteen, there it was three fifteen, a nice house in a nice neighborhood. Carefully Roy turned into the drive and parked the car. He smoothed out his windblown hair and stepped out of the car. He picked up the rose that Helen had gotten for him, careful not to prick himself on the thorns. The door was only a couple of steps from the drive, which was the best thing or Roy would have never made it. Cautiously, he rang the doorbell.

The afternoon had sped by for Becca; she had gotten home and barely had time to shower and change. She felt grand and her outfit showed it. The knee length navy skirt fit nicely and the light blue silk blouse hugged her breasts. She was fastening an Indian style necklace on when she heard a knock at the door. Quickly she slipped on her pumps, smoothed out her skirt and blouse and headed for the door. Calming herself with a deep breath, Becca opened the door and greeted her date.

Roy froze with fear as the door opened. Had it been a dream last night? He could not believe that he had actually asked her out and she had said yes. Becca opened the door and looked at Roy with the same expression of trepidation on her face. Both of them did the cod fish routine, mouths agape and sucking air. After about ten seconds, Roy smiled and handed the rose to Becca. Taking the rose, she inhaled the fragrance and mouthed the words thank you. Turning to the table beside the door she picked up her purse and shut the door.

Roy extended his arm, which Becca took graciously. They walked arm in arm to the far side of the car, where Roy opened the door and helped her in. He could not help but stare as she swung her long legs into the car. The car started with a roar and soon they were back out on the interstate heading for Chicago.

"Where to for dinner on Friday night in Chicago?" Becca inquired.

"How about Italian?"

"Sounds good to me, but where?'

"You will see. Now tell me a little more about this teaching project you do for the university." Roy turned the conversation away from the location of dinner and back to her, partly so it would be a surprise and partly so he could hear her talk.

"I go around and teach Native American culture to schools in Illinois and Iowa. They are half-day seminars and we use all kind of multimedia to describe the life of a Plains tribe in the seventeen and eighteen hundreds," Becca explained. Over the next half hour she told Roy about her work. The more she talked the more animated she became. Roy watched as the energy and excitement flowed from her. The wind caught her red hair and swept it back like a prairie fire. Curtis shook his head slightly and grinned at the sight of this lady next to him. She was every bit the wild Indian pony that she talked about.

"What?" Becca asked as she saw him smiling at her.

"Nothing, just wondering what you would look like dressed in a squaw's dress instead of stockings and heels," Roy replied. He spoke the truth but inside new questions began to form. For now he stifled these questions and enjoyed the ride. For the next hour Roy and Becca talked each searching the others eyes and heart. Roy listened as she told him of her childhood and life in rural Illinois. Then he took her hand and talked of his days in the Marines and showing cattle. All too quickly the signs of the city came into view. Becca rested her hand on Roy's leg as he drove through the dense Chicago traffic.

They pulled up to the front of the office building and stopped. The valet rushed over and opened the door. Roy tossed him the keys as he walked around the car.

"Park it in my spot, will you please? Just lock the keys in it, I have my remote entry."

"Yes, sir. Is there anything else you need tonight, Mr. Curtis?" the attendant asked.

"No that will be all, thanks." Roy took Becca's hand and led her around the corner of the building where the stretch limousine was waiting. The driver opened the door, letting them get in.

"Where to?" the driver asked.

"Only one place, Vinnie's on 82$^{nd}$ and LaSalle," Roy said. The driver nodded that she knew the place and soon they were off to dinner. The ride through the city was quiet and Becca leaned against him and stretched out her long legs, her skirt hiked up as she did, but she made no attempt to pull it down. Her perfume was having an intoxicating effect on Roy as he watched her. Becca leaned against Roy's shoulder and snuggled up against him. As they talked, Becca idly traced her fingers across the back of his hand. His fingers found their way to her cheek and he could feel the heat generated from her skin. He put his finger on her chin and turned her face toward his. Slowly and delicately his lips touched hers. As if in a dream they kissed, tenderly and lovingly as the dreams and memories of the past met the reality of today.

All too soon they reached the restaurant, Roy was tempted to tell the driver to go around the block one more time, but once again manners took over. Becca got out of the limo and shook her head in disbelief as she looked at the crowd waiting to get in. They wouldn't be able to eat for at least an hour and she didn't care whether he was the cowboy of her dreams or not, she was hungry and wanted to eat. She would take a burger rather than stand in line. She started to say something when Roy motioned her to follow him. He walked up to the hostess and handed her a card. She looked at it, smiled and headed to the back of the restaurant.

The hostess had been gone not more than a minute when a loud booming voice hollered, "Hey, Curtis, what's happening, man?"

Becca turned around and standing in front of her was a man the size of a bear. Vinnie Blanchard stood six foot four and weighed every bit of two hundred seventy-five pounds. The two men embraced like old friends and then stood back and laughed.

"It's good to see you, Chief," Roy said. "It has been way too long."

"I had given you up for dead, except that you're too ugly to die."

"Not half as ugly as you."

"That's not what the women say." The big man laughed again. "A table for two and a bottle of the best." He spoke as one used to giving orders.

"This way, and your lovely companion's name?"

"Not that I should introduce you to her, you'll just try to steal her away. Becca Davidson meet Vincent Blanchard, former Fire Chief, Fallbrook Volunteer Fire Department. Vinnie meet Rebecca Davidson, lecturer and author."

"My pleasure," Vinnie said leading them to their table. The place was packed, but in the back corner was a secluded table for two. The waiter brought the wine and took their orders. While they waited for the food, they drank wine and talked.

"So how does Roy Curtis rate special treatment at one of the hottest spots in Chicago?" Becca asked as she looked around at the crowd and the decor of an Old Italian restaurant.

"The Chief and I go back a long time. I met him when I was stationed out at Camp Pendleton just after college. There was a brush fire and the Marines were called out to help fight it. Vinnie was the chief in charge and for three days straight we stood side by side and fought that fire." Roy took a sip of wine as he relived that event. "Vinnie will tell you I saved his life and I will tell you I was running scared and tripped over a root and bumped into him. Either way the burning tree just missed him as it fell. He ended up with a burned hand and a bump on the head, but I ended up with a life-long friend."

Becca stared at Roy as he told the story, listening to every word he said. Roy felt Becca's foot begin to play with his leg and she winked when his hand took hers. The food was marvelous, the chicken fettuccini was seasoned just right and the wine was excellent. They finished off dinner with a piece of cheesecake. Vinnie met them and walked them to the door.

"When you dump this loser," Vinnie kidded to Becca as they left the restaurant, "you come see me, OK?"

"Thanks for nothing, Vinnie. Besides Martha wouldn't approve," Roy jabbed back. "It was good to see you again."

"Keep your line primed," Vinnie told them as they exited through the door.

"Simper Fi," Roy replied. Turning to Becca, "I told the driver to meet us up by the lake in about an hour. Would you care to go for a walk?"

"I would love to."

Arm in arm they walked down the street. Like two old friends they fell in step and drifted along looking at the shops. Roy stopped just before reaching the beach and took Becca's hands and looked her in the eyes. Her eyes once again sparkled like sapphires and their light plunged deep into Roy's heart. It wasn't just passion but something deeper and hotter. The power of her eyes matched her stature; eye to eye they stood, looking deep into each other's soul trying to read the other's thoughts. Finally Roy had to look away.

"Seems like we always end up at the beach," Becca said slightly flushed by the thoughts that were flowing through her mind. Not wanting Roy to see, she looked out over the darkness of the lake.

"It does seem that way doesn't it."

"Maybe I'll run out into the water again and let you carry me back to shore."

"No." Roy said matter-of-factly.

"No?" Becca asked in a mocking tone. She turned and took a step towards the water, before Becca could take a second step Roy grabbed her arm and spun her around. He pulled her close and kissed her hard on the mouth. The kiss ignited the flames of passion and lust in Roy's soul. The young lustful side of Roy wanted to take her out onto the beach and make love to her like there was no tomorrow, but the mature older man inside of him told him that there was a tomorrow and if he gave into the lustful side then the enchantment that they had would be gone. Reluctantly he listened to the old man and broke the kiss.

Releasing one hand, Roy led the way back toward the limo. Becca leaned her head against his shoulder and held onto his arm with both hands. As they slowly walked, they were serenaded by the chirp of crickets. A light breeze brought the smell of the lake to the shore. Silence ruled as neither wanted to give up the specialness that they felt. The limo was waiting at the end of the walk when they got there. Roy handed the driver directions and a note just before she shut the door behind them.

The ride back to Becca's townhouse was calm and tranquil. Roy switched on some smooth jazz and sat back to relax. Kicking her shoes off, Becca curled her legs underneath herself and leaned against Roy. The combination of the music, the warmth of her body and the smell of her perfume caused Roy to nod off. Becca snuggled up tightly against him and drifted off to dream land too. It seem like the trip had only begun when the driver awoke them via the intercom. Roy walked her to the door. At the door, Becca turned and embraced him. Backing up slightly she looked him in the eyes and whispered drowsily.

"You know, I think you stole something of mine tonight."

"And what might that be?" he asked incredulously.

"My heart," she whispered.

"Then it is a fair trade because I gave a piece of mine to you."

"I will guard it with my life," she said, kissing him once more on the lips. A long embrace followed that neither wanted to end. Knowing that they must, Becca slowly let go.

"Thank you for a wonderful evening."

"You're welcome, how about next Saturday night? A play maybe?" Roy asked.

"I would love it. Call me with details. You have my cell phone and email, use either or both." Becca said suddenly wide awake and full of life. "I can't wait."

"Good night then." Roy's lips met hers and he quickly ended the kiss or he would never make it back to Chicago. *Maybe that wouldn't be so bad*, he thought as he walked back to the car. He turned and looked back at the door. Becca was standing just where he had left her. Roy blew her a kiss and ducked into the car. The passenger area was filled with the scent of her perfume and Roy knew it would be a long ride back to the office.

Becca walked in the house and flopped on the couch, exhausted and a little bewildered. Two days ago, she had been a confident and independent teacher of history with no need for men in her life. Now here she was almost aching with desire for a man she had known for just over twenty-four hours. What was it that made him so different from the others that had hit on her? How had he penetrated the wall that she had put up around her with such ease? Was she that desperate for love? She didn't think so, but there had to be a reason.

Pushing herself up from the sofa, Becca headed to the bedroom. *A nice shower and a good night's rest will clear my head*, she thought. She stood in the shower and let the cool water cascade down over her body. More than once since her ex-husband had run off had she stood under the mist of a shower and let the water drive the loneliness away. Tonight though it the feeling was different, it was brought on by having felt the warmth of a man's soul again. Thoroughly relaxed Becca toweled off and pulled an oversized T-shirt on and crawled into bed. She tossed and turned and dreamed of the man in the dream catcher. The face was starting to take the shape of the face of Roy Curtis.

Roy leaned back and tried to get some sleep on the way back to Chicago, but rest would not come. The fragrance of her perfume would not release its grip from him. The memory of the silkiness of her lips when they kissed and the passion that passed between them stirred the embers of his soul that had been dormant since that fateful day many years before. Those little sparks of love and passion that he had guarded so closely were now in danger of getting loose and bursting into a full fledged fire.

The Z4 eased into the parking space around two in the morning.

Roy had been tempted to have the chauffeur drop him off but then he would have been without his car and would have had to get a ride back to the office. Tomorrow was Saturday and he wanted to get out to the farm as quickly as possible. Even after only four hours sleep, Roy was up and ready to go. Every bit as refreshed as he had been the previous day, he headed for the farm. The drive to the Seven C Cattle Co. seem surprisingly short today, even so he couldn't help but think about Becca and the previous two evenings. Thoughts of her danced through his head; he remembered the smell of her perfume, how she held her dress up and stood in the water, even her laugh.

In what seemed no time he pulled up the gravel driveway to the big farmhouse. It was mid-morning and Maria would be in the kitchen preparing lunch for all the help. Roy bound onto the back porch and pushed the screen door wide open.

"Gooood morning!" Roy hollered as he entered the kitchen. "Smells tasty, must have known I was coming for lunch."

"If I had known you were coming for lunch, I'd have burnt it for sure," Maria said with a smile. "My aren't we happy this morning? Oh, Mr. Justin said he was going to be over at the calving sheds and could use some help if you was fit to stand. Looks to me like you is, so get."

"Yes, ma'am," Roy bowed in fake horror. "I'm leaving right now." Roy headed to the mud room and changed into his work clothes. Pushing cattle on a horse was fun, but tagging calves was down right messy. Getting knocked over by some overly protective cow was not a good way to stay clean. Roy traded his Z4 for the pickup and drove over to the calving sheds. Actually it was one long barn divided into six pens, sixteen by sixteen square. The barn was designed so that first calf heifers and cows that calved in the winter could be watched. In the summer the cows had their calves in a ten acre pasture next to the barn. Today Justin and a few of the hands were putting tags in their ears before turning them and the cows out into the main pasture.

"Good morning, Curtis." Justin Roberts waved at him as he came in the barn. "You here to show us how it's done today?"

"How many you tagging this morning?" Roy said as he looked into one of the holding pens.

"Twenty-seven. Most of these cows will get moved over to the west pasture with Sonar." Sonar was the son of the national champion polled Hereford bull and from the looks of things his calves were going to be just as good.

"Well, let's get started. Hand me a halter." Curtis opened the gate to the pen and stepped in with the calves. Though he could throw a lariat as well as anybody, he preferred a rope halter when working closely with young calves. The rest of the day, except for a break for lunch, was spent catching and tagging calves. After they were all tagged the rest of the help herded the cows and calves over to the west pasture. The farm had been set up with driveways between the pastures so once the cows headed down the proper drive one person could move them with ease.

"You seem in a good mood today," Justin said as the two of them sat on the tailgate of the truck. Each had a mug of iced tea and was enjoying the afternoon sunshine.

"I had a pretty good week. It has been a long time since I had one that good," Roy said as he thought of Becca and her kiss.

"Glad to hear it. Maybe you'll have a couple more and be tolerable for a change."

"To you too," Curtis grumbled and took another swig of tea. Smiling as he did.

# Chapter 11

It was not that Becca really expected him to call, but he had sounded sincere when he had mentioned the play on Saturday night. So it was with mixed emotions when she saw the e-mail from him pop up on her computer screen. Hesitantly she clicked on the message and began to read.

Dear Becca,

Please accept my apologies for not calling. I have been extremely busy at work and have not been getting home until late. Since I forgot to ask when it would be appropriate to call, I thought I should e-mail you. I have tickets for the theater on Saturday night if you would like to go. I will pick you up around 4:00 p.m. Let me know one way or the other.

I am sorry for how impersonal this letter is. I really had a great time last weekend and am looking forward to seeing you soon.

Respectfully yours,
Roy

Becca's temper flared for a second as she read the letter. How dare he assume that he can just e-mail and expect her to jump at his invitation. She banged out a nasty reply, wishing she had time to tell him in person how she felt. Suddenly she stopped typing, the irony of it hitting her smack dab in the face. If she didn't have time to call him how should he be expected to? Clearing the reply she started over and graciously accepted the invitation to the play.

The limousine pulled up in front of her townhouse at exactly four in the afternoon. Becca took one last look in the mirror and headed to the door. She opened the door just as Roy was getting ready to knock and just about got clobbered in the face by his big hand.
"Excuse me, I am so sorry," Roy apologized profusely.
"No, it's my fault; I keep forgetting that gentlemen come to the door for their date," Becca said somewhat embarrassed by her breach in protocol.
"May I?" Curtis asked, extending his arm to Becca.
"Thank you. It will be my pleasure," she said as she wrapped her arm around his. Together, like a perfect couple, they walked to the waiting limo. The ride to the theater was uneventful and they spent the time talking about the past week and what had gone on in their lives. The play was excellent and Becca leaned over against Roy and wondered what it be like to be the leading lady and have the hero come and take her off into sunset. After the play, Roy took Becca to a small diner for dessert. Becca ordered a sundae and Roy got a piece of banana cream pie. Roy ate his pie slowly watching Becca as she ate hers. Becca saw him staring at her and broke his trance by putting a blob of whipped cream on his nose. Roy jerked away but the white dollop stayed right where it was. Becca laughed as he wiped the cream off, Roy had his revenge as he put a spoonful of cream on her chin. Both laughed so loud that the other customers turned and looked, but neither cared and just kept laughing. Passersby would have wondered if they were drunk as they walked to the limo arm in arm, because the laughter was causing them to stumble.

Once in the back of the limo, Becca caught her breath and wiped the tears of laughter from the corners of her eyes. When the two of them finally quit laughing, Becca looked at Roy and a sudden urge swept over her. Reaching over with her long fingers she turned Roy's face towards her and kissed him hard and fast on the lips. Roy reacted quickly and pulled her to him and let the passion flow as they kissed.

"Wow!" was all Roy could say as their lips parted. "Not that I am complaining, but what brought that on?"

"I am not sure, but I think I could use some more." With that Becca planted another long, wet kiss which Roy readily accepted and returned with an equal amount of energy. Roy allowed his hands to roam from the small of her back to the top of her hair. The softness of her hair sent fireworks through his heart and he fought hard for self control. Breaking the kiss, Roy took a deep breath and looked Becca straight into her deep blue eyes. A full sixty seconds passed before either said a word.

"It has been a long time since I have done this romance thing," Roy said with a hint of insecurity in his voice.

"Me too, but I think we are doing okay," Becca agreed.

"I am not sure I can live up to your expectations," Roy felt his emotional wall starting to rise around him again.

"I am sure you can, right now my expectations of men are pretty low."

"Gee thanks, and besides, my schedule at work won't let me...."

"Shhh...." Becca touched his lips with her fingers. "Right now I am having more fun and am happier than I have been in years. So if we can see each other once every couple of weeks and talk or email in between I will be happy. Understand?"

"I think I understand."

"Good. Now if you would like, you can raise my expectations a little with another kiss."

"My pleasure," Roy answered as his lips met hers for another long kiss. The remainder of the ride Becca spent curled up next to Roy. The short way up her townhouse drive seemed even shorter as neither wanted to part. For an instant Becca thought about inviting him in, but stopped short of asking. Roy sensed her hesitation and responded to the unasked question.

"I've told you that you look good in the moonlight and that someday I will see you in the morning light. We will both know when it is right so don't worry OK? Remember you said I held your heart and I told you I would take care of it and I will." Roy gave her one more kiss and a long embrace before saying good-bye. The ride back to Chicago was long and lonely for Roy. His heart longed for this beautiful lady that had entered his life. So why was he holding back? Why couldn't he let go? It was different than the few flings he had experienced over the years. Those had been strictly to satisfy his physical needs and though he had said words they had been lip service only and not from deep inside of him like now.

"Take a look what the delivery man just dropped off," Pam said as she held up a large arrangement of flowers. "I wonder who these could be for."

"Aren't they beautiful?" Becca said as she took them from Pam and set them on the credenza. The fragrance of the roses and baby's breath seemed to fill the whole room. Carefully Becca took the card from the holder.

"Who are they from?" Pam inquired. "I bet I know."

"They are from Roy," Becca said. She felt slightly flushed at the thought of him. Flipping the card open she read the note.

Becca,
I had a wonderful time last Saturday night.
You have changed my life forever.

The keeper of your heart,
Roy

Tears welled up in Becca's eyes. She bit her lip to keep from crying. Pam saw the expression on her face and asked "Are you OK? Is anything wrong?"

"I'm fine, just fine." The tears began to flow down her cheeks as she answered. It had been so long since anyone had sent her flowers or a gift that her emotions just let go. For fifteen minutes she looked at the card and flowers. Just about the time Becca thought she had them under control another wave of tears started. Quickly Pam shut the door and locked it, so that no one would walk in.

"Pretty special guy, huh?" Pam commented as she handed Becca a tissue.

"You would not believe, Pam, how special, besides being good looking and fairly rich he is a gentleman through and through." Becca sniffled and dried the last of the tears. "Remember when you laughed at him wearing a cowboy tuxedo to the opening and I said I thought he was genuine. Well I know he is. That cowboy code of manners that everyone talks about, Roy Curtis is the personification of that code. Somehow I am going to keep him."

"Only if he wants to be kept."

"He wants to; he just doesn't know it yet."

"Be careful, Becca."

"I will Pam, I will," Becca answered as she sat down at the computer. Roy had said he would be out of the office the first part of the week and to e-mail him if she wanted to. Well, she wanted to and bad. Clicking on one of the greeting cards sites, Becca e-mailed a thank you card to him.

Over the next several weeks, Roy and Becca's relationship took on an electronic dimension. They still saw each other on the weekends and Roy would call Becca every other day or so. But every day Roy would send her an e-mail to begin her day, most days they were just a quick note hello or an e-card. They had been seeing each other for a month, when Roy sat down to write his morning note. Today the words seem to roll off his fingers and on to the screen. Roy read the note over and over again. He hoped it said what he felt and not more or less. Did he sound silly? Would Becca think him a fool? He sincerely hoped not. With fear and trepidation he hit the send button.

By the end of the first week Becca had gotten into the habit of checking her e-mail first thing in the morning for a card from Roy. But this e-mail file was longer than normal and Becca hoped it was not a "Dear Jane" letter. So she opened it with as much fear as Roy had when he sent it. Pam walked in as Becca finished reading the letter. Becca was dabbing her eyes, so when Pam gave her a quizzical look Becca motioned her over to look at the screen:

My Dear Becca,
When I try to talk to you, I seem to get tongue tied. So I am writing this in the hopes that I may express to you the feelings that I find growing in my heart for you. My life that was once void of emotion is now full and overflowing. Not a day goes by that I don't think of you. The hours of the week both fly and linger. They fly by as I realize that I can only see you for a short time each week, They linger and creep by as my anticipation grows for that short time that I may gaze into your sapphire blue eyes and listen to the melodious tones of your voice.
If I were a songwriter, I would write a song to describe how I feel. Then the whole world could listen to my heart as it beats in anticipation of your kiss on my lips.
Thank you again for a great weekend.

Until I see you again,
I will keep your heart safe.
Roy

"Oh wow!" Pam exclaimed, grabbing a Kleenex also, "Does he always write like that?"
"No, this is a first," Becca replied, "but I always suspected it was in there somewhere. It is just the cowboy in him."
"Well just make sure he doesn't get away."

On a late August morning, Becca was in her office working on her program for the coming school year. Pam was due back in the office on Monday from her trip to the Rockies, and there would be a lot of work to be completed before the fall semester began. She had just finished a tall glass of iced tea and was getting ready to head down to the lounge for a refill when the phone rang.

"This is Becca," she answered after the second ring. "How may I help you?"

"Hey, beautiful."

Becca's face lit up like the morning sun as she recognized Roy's voice. "Hi, Roy, what's up?"

"Well, I happen to have the whole weekend off and I was wondering if you would like to go to Lake Wawasee and then see the ranch?" Roy inquired.

"Oh, I have been wanting to see your farm for weeks, I would love to go."

"Great. Can you meet me here at the office and then we could ride out together."

"I can get off around noon tomorrow, so I can be there around three," Becca replied.

"OK, see you then. By the way, can you ride?"

"It has been a while," Becca said, "but I think I can hold my own."

"Super, it should be a great weekend," Roy exclaimed. "Don't forget to pack a swimsuit. See you tomorrow."

"See you tomorrow."

"Oh, Becca, I miss you."

"I miss you, too. Bye."

"Bye."

Becca hung up the phone and leaned back against the desk. She willed her breathing to slow. Why was it every time they talked her heart fluttered like a schoolgirl's? Well she had better get to work if she was going to be gone all weekend.

# Chapter 12

Becca pulled her Jeep Cherokee into the parking garage at exactly three in the afternoon. She had called Roy just before she got there, so the parking attendant had let her right in and Roy was waiting to direct her into his parking spot. His Z4 was idling smoothly and pointed toward the exit. A quick kiss hello and then they transferred her bags to the back seat. Roy helped Becca into the roadster and then hopped across the trunk and into the car. Once again he left the garage a little faster than he should have, but it was a great summer afternoon and he felt like flying.

The one hundred twenty mile trip from downtown Chicago to the farm took just under two hours. Once out of the city and on Highway 6, Roy opened up the BMW and sped along the country road. Roy pointed out local sights as they passed through northern Indiana, slowing only when they had to pass a black buggy with an Amish family heading home from the market. Becca watch the countryside slip by the car as she enjoyed the running commentary of who lived where and what.

Maria saw the plume of dust trailing the Z4 as it roared down the gravel lane. Smiling she returned to preparing dinner for two. Roy had called her this morning and asked her to get the master suite and the guest room ready, because he was bringing a lady guest to spend the weekend. Immediately Maria had aired out the upstairs room and set about fixing a dinner for two.

Picking up Becca's bags, Roy led the way to the house. They entered through the back door and into the kitchen, where the smell of Maria's cooking filled the room. Roy gave his housekeeper a hug and introduced her and Becca.

"Maria," Roy began, "this is Becca Davidson. Becca, this is my housekeeper, Maria Gonzalez."

"Maria," Becca said, as she took Maria's hand. "It is a pleasure to finally meet you and taste your fabulous cooking that Roy always raves about."

"Senor Curtis," Maria replied, switching into her teasing Spanglish. "He talks way too much."

"Oh does he now?" she asked, winking at Roy. "We will have to have a talk before I leave and compare notes."

"Well not before we eat," Roy interrupted, "because a condemned man deserves his last meal."

"Roy, you take the lady's things up to the guest room and when you return, your supper will be ready. Becca will you help me set the table?" Maria said.

Supper consisted of baked steak and gravy, fried potatoes and green beans, a loaf of fresh bread and lots of iced tea. Leave it to Maria to impress even with a Friday supper, Roy thought. They ate in the dining room and Becca could not get over the subdued elegance of the old farmhouse.

"Did your family build this house?" Becca asked.

"My great-grandfather had it built in the late eighteen hundreds." Roy answered as he buttered a slice of fresh bread. "Each generation has lived here since. When I am gone…." Roy's voice trailed off as memories of Jacki and Brent rushed in. The rest of the meal was eaten in silence. Becca wondered what she had done wrong.

After supper, Roy seemed back to the person Becca had come to know. Laughing, he took her on a tour of the house, showing each room and the antiques and memorabilia that filled them. The trophy room thoroughly amazed Becca, trophies and banners from every major show in the country lined the walls. Some were for the cattle, others the Quarter Horses; Becca studied the banners and the pictures that were with them. Pictures from the early fifties contained Roy's grandfather. Then his father joined the picture. In the seventies, a young Roy joined the pictures and all three generations were in the picture with the National Champion Bull. A picture from the late nineties showed a lovely lady and a young boy had joined the group. When she turned to ask Roy who it was, Becca found herself all alone.

Roy was standing in the hall, when Becca exited the trophy room. The shadow that Becca had seen at supper had returned to Curtis' face and she decided not to pursue the identity of the lady in the picture. She took Roy's hand and led him to the next room. The next room was definitely not being used for the same purpose as when Great-grandfather Curtis had the house built. Roy had converted the parlor into a multimedia room, three elevated rows of navy blue theater recliners stretched across the room. The far side of the room housed a 60" plasma TV screen, with built in shelving containing the surround sound system.

"Now this is cool," Becca said. "How about we watch a movie? I bet it sounds great in here."

"Yeah, it is pretty impressive," Roy commented, slightly relieved to be finished with the house tour and the memories that were being dredged up. "Blood and guts, or chick flick?"

"I know this sounds funny coming from me, but maybe a western?"

"I have just the movie." Just then the phone rang. Curtis answered on the second ring. Becca tried to figure out the conversation, all she could hear were "yeahs" and "gotchas."

"See you tomorrow at Barrington's. Bye." With that Roy abruptly hung up the phone. Turning to Becca, he spoke. "That was Justin, my farm manager. Everyone is meeting around eleven at the Barrington's place. Looks like there will be four couples, you should like everybody. How about a piece of pie while we watch the movie? I think Maria fixed a blackberry pie this afternoon."

Before Becca could answer, Roy had left the room and just as quickly he returned with two pieces of blackberry pie a la mode. Handing them to Becca, Roy walked over to the shelves that contained all the DVD's and selected one. After popping in *Hidalgo*, he settled next to Becca to enjoy. The movie about a long distance rider and his horse was just what the doctor ordered and soon Becca was curled up next to Roy, her head on his chest and his big arm around her. Before long the stress of a busy week began to retreat from their bodies and their breathing more relaxed and deeper. Neither Roy nor Becca saw the ending credits as they retreated to dream world.

Becca awoke first around two in the morning, and gently shook Roy to awaken him. Groggily the couple stretched and then headed upstairs, leaving the empty plates for Maria to clean up in the morning. Opening the door to the guest room, Roy showed Becca the room and the bathroom. He took her in his arms and kissed her long and hard, tempted to invite her to his room. Roy elected not to, because if Becca was half as sleepy as he was, they would be asleep before the first kiss. Roy shut the door and headed to his room, within five minutes of shutting the door, his eyes were shut and dreams of a beautiful redhead were filling his head.

Roy awoke later than usual and by the time he had finished showering and dressing for a day at the lake it was almost ten. He headed across the hall to the guest room to see if Becca was awake. The door was ajar so Roy knocked and then entered an empty room. Backing out he headed down the stairs. He heard sounds coming from the kitchen so Curtis made his way there.

Maria and Becca were standing at the kitchen island making sandwiches. Becca looked up and blew Roy a good morning kiss, which Roy promptly returned. Becca's hair was in a ponytail and her sunglasses were up on her head. She wore a bright blue mid-thigh beach cover up. Roy was curious as to her swimsuit, but all he could see was a pair of purple strings circling her neck.

"Good morning, sleepyhead." Becca smiled at him. "Iced tea is in the fridge if you want some. Do you want anything else?"

"No tea is enough. What's with all the sandwiches?" Roy asked as he filled his glass with tea.

"Halsey called last night and wanted to know if I could make some," Maria said, referring to Halsey Barrington, the hostess of today's outing. "I told her no problemo and Becca was drinking a cup of tea when I got here and volunteered to help. We're just about finished."

"Good. It takes about twenty minutes to get to the Barrington's on Ogden Point. We'll take the truck today."

Becca finished the sandwiches and closed the cooler. Roy grabbed the cooler and the couple headed out the back door. Curtis put the large cooler in the bed of the truck. Becca tossed the orange duffle bag containing all the towels and lotions in the back also and climbed into the big Ford pickup. Backing the truck around Roy pointed the truck down the drive and they were on their way. A quick trip on Highway 6 and then a turn south to Lake Wawasee, Roy pulled into what appeared to be the back of a large house. There were two cars and another pickup parked in the drive.

"All the houses around here face the lake, so the backs face the street," Roy said. "It looks like we are the last ones here. Here is the duffle bag."

Curtis led the way around the side of the house to the patio and dock area. The patio was a clay tiled area with teak furniture, lined with plants and vines covered the trellis archway that led down to the dock. It looked like the other six were enjoying a pre-party drink, because alcohol was prohibited on the boat.

"Let me introduce you to everybody," Roy started the introductions, pointing to the three guys on the dock working on the boat. "Hey, guys, this is Becca. The tall guy with the buzzed red hair is John Kilkenny, the one with the ball cap is Justin Roberts my manager, and the blonde headed dude with the sunglasses is our host Geoffrey Barrington."

A various assortment of grunts, hellos and howdys came from the boat and then the three guys disappeared back down into the engine area. Roy set the cooler on the patio and headed down to the boat, completely forgetting to introduce Becca to the ladies sitting on the patio.

"Hi, I am Halsey, I am Geoff's wife," the tall thin blonde greeted her. "This is Lisa, Justin's wife, and Jessica Kilkenny."

"Nice to meet you, I am so looking forward to get out on the lake. What seems to be the problem with the boat?"

Lisa answered the inquiry, "According to Justin, there is a problem with the fuel line, but none of them are mechanics so it could be just about anything. So we will just sip drinks until they give up."

"You don't sound so hopeful about swimming today."

"Absolutely not," Halsey lamented.

"Well then I guess I probably better go bust some male egos and get the boat fixed," Becca said as she got up and walked down to the boat.

"Excuse me, gentlemen, let me have a look," she said, picking up the work light and looking down into the compartment.

"Oh guys, we better let her have a little room," Roy said, "I think she knows what she is doing." Sure enough within ten minutes, the huge engine sputtered, rumbled, and then purred to life. Becca stood up and smiled, her hands and dress were covered with dirt and grease. Still smiling, she walked back up the sidewalk to the patio, kissed Roy on the cheek and then looked at Halsey.

"You wouldn't have a place were a poor, dirty girl could clean up do you?" Putting on her best poor lil' ol' me expression.

"Sure, Becca, follow me. And I think I might have something else for you to wear also." Halsey led the way inside to the bathroom. Becca pulled the beach dress over her head and proceeded to wash her hands and face. Halsey returned to bathroom carrying some clothes.

"Here I brought you a sarong to wear. Oh, wow," Halsey exclaimed, looking at Becca standing there in her purple bikini. "Maybe I had better get a shirt for you instead."

"Do I look that bad?" Becca asked incredulously.

"Oh no, not by any means, but if the guys get a look at you before we get out of the channel, they are liable to wreck the boat," Halsey replied.

"Give me that thing then," Becca said taking the sarong. "There is more than one way to wear one of these. I learned this during *South Pacific* from the drama instructor at the school where I used to work." With that she took the multi-color piece of cloth and tied it just under her armpit and made a strapless type cover up from it.

"I think that will work," Halsey said. "Let's get going. The boys will be itching to get on the lake now that "they" fixed the boat. Roy had told us you were a mechanic and a good one it looks like."

Together they left the house and headed to the pontoon boat, where sure enough, the rest were waiting. John extended his hand and helped the pair on board. As soon as the ladies were seated, Justin and Roy untied the dock lines and pushed off. Easing the throttle forward, Geoff piloted the thirty-footer with ease down the channel. Becca watched the different boats slip by as they headed out on the lake.

"I think we will cruise for a while before we drop anchor at the sand bar, so sit back and enjoy." With that he pushed the throttle to half and the big engine pushed the boat forward with increasing speed. For the next hour, they toured the lake and munched on the snacks that everyone had brought. Geoff served as tour guide telling who live were and what famous or infamous person had owned what house.

Finally they met a large gathering of boats in the middle of the lake. Halsey told Becca that this was the sand bar and basically the local swimming hole for the lake. The water was just four feet deep and was perfect for playing in the lake. Positioning the pontoon between a couple of small speedboats, Geoff dropped anchor and pronounced it was swimming time. Taking a run to the rear he dove off the platform, then swam about ten yards from the boat, stood and waved to the others. John, Roy and Justin joined Geoff in the lake. The four women looked at each other and nodded and headed to the diving platform. Jessica was the first to lose her sarong and the pink tankini solicited a couple of wolf whistles. Lisa pulled off her cover up and the catcalls were just as loud even though she wore a black one-piece racing suit. Becca's purple string bikini caused the loudest noise, especially from Roy as she did a sexy show of removing her sarong. Halsey's boy-cut bikini with a yellow and red print caused the eyes to turn equally. Taking each other's hands the four ladies stepped off the platform and into the water. For the next couple of hours the four couples played and swam. They joined in a pickup beach ball volleyball game at the floating net in the middle of the sandbar.

Finally Lisa put an end to the frolicking saying that she wanted to work on her tan and headed to the boat. The other women agreed and joined her.

"It sure would be nice if I had someone big and strong to rub lotion on my back," Becca said as she passed Roy going to the pontoon boat. She blew him a kiss and took off with Roy following right behind. Drying off on the platform, Becca and Roy climbed up to the upper sundeck, where Lisa was already laying out. Becca lay down on her stomach, untied her top straps and closed her eyes. She purred slightly as Roy's big hands worked the lotion on her back and legs. All Becca could think of was back on the beach with Pam in the Dells and how she thought a man rubbing lotion on her would be perfect and how perfect this was. When Roy finished, he gave her a light peck on the cheek and headed down to the lower deck.

The other two ladies took their places on the sundeck and untied or pulled up tops to maximize the sun. As they tanned, they began to talk. Lisa asked about how Becca met Roy, they had heard Roy's version and wanted to compare. Talk went from Roy to Geoff to JP to Justin as each lady told of meeting her man. As Lisa talked of meeting Justin at a cattle show, Becca remembered the picture with the lady and child in it and asked Lisa about it. The question caused all three heads to look up at Becca.

"That's his late wife," Halsey said. "You mean you didn't know Roy had been married before?"

"Oh, I knew he had been married," Becca said, "but he never told me about her or that she had died."

"She and their son were killed in an auto accident about ten years ago," Jessica stated.

"I can't believe he didn't tell me," replied Becca, a little hurt by the secret that had been kept from her. "Maybe this whole thing has been just a summer fling."

"Didn't you say you were going to go riding tomorrow?" Halsey asked.

"Yeah, but if I am only a fling...."

Halsey cut her off. "Relax, Becca, you're no summer fling. As far as I know, you are the first lady he has ever taken riding on the ranch. So it is pretty safe to say you are very special to him."

"If you say so," Becca said, still not quite sure.

"Well we had better rotate," Lisa instructed, "because if you are going riding tomorrow you don't want to be burned to a crisp."

"Hey, Jessica," Halsey looked over at her friend, "think we ought to take Becca to the Barbee tonight for supper?"

"That sounds great," Jess replied and then looked over at Becca. "Do you have plans for dinner?"

"I don't think I do," was Becca's response to the question.

"Great, let me talk to the guys." Halsey leaned over the sundeck and spoke to the guys who were playing cards, oblivious to the conversation going on above them. "Hey, Geoff, what do think of the Barbee for supper?"

The four guys looked at each other and as one answered yes. Justin grabbed his ever-present cellphone and called for reservations for seven-thirty that evening. Geoff hoisted the anchor and started the engine.

"How about a slow cruise back to the house?" Geoff hollered up at Halsey.

"OK, see you when we get to the dock."

Geoff started the big pontoon across the lake. Everyone else stretched out in the sun, the women on the top sundeck and the men down below. The steady roll of the boat rocked each of them to sleep as they soaked in the summer sun. All too soon they were awakened by the change of pitch in the boat's engine as Geoff began to maneuver the pontoon into its berth. Justin and John tossed out the bumper buoys and Roy jumped ashore to catch the lines. Once the boat was secure the ladies climbed down from the sundeck, sarongs and cover-ups in place, and helped unload the boat. Geoff and John put the covers on and Roy and Justin carried coolers up to the house.

"Looks like we have about enough time for everyone to go home and clean up before dinner," Geoff said, looking at his watch. "We have seven-thirty reservations."

With that everyone said their good byes and headed for their vehicles. The ride back to the ranch was quiet; Roy attributed it to Becca being tired, when in reality she was contemplating her future with a man who hadn't told her about his late wife.

The Barbee Hotel had been built in the early 1900s and during Prohibition had been frequented by Al Capone himself. The place had that nostalgic atmosphere that so many wannabe hot spots craved. The food was excellent and they all laughed and carried on as they went from course to course. The last of the coffee had been drunk and they were thinking of leaving when the announcement was made that the dance floor was open. Each couple made their way to the floor and began to dance. They had just finished a line dance in which Roy politely sat out, saying he didn't want to embarrass himself by his lack of coordination. In reality he just wanted to watch Becca move, which she did, Roy thought, with style and grace. A slow jazz number started and Becca came and took his hand. Any doubts about Roy had retreated to the back of her mind and she glowed in his arms as the danced. The ride home this time was also quiet but there was no doubt in Becca's mind, just a growing affection for the man she was leaning against. They kissed long and passionately before heading off to their bedrooms, each wondering if the other would have minded spending the night together.

# Chapter 13

Roy woke early the next morning, and after a quick shower and shave, he headed to his closet. What should he wear? True, he was a real life cowboy and could ride with the best, but he didn't want to look like a drifter neither did he want to look too dudish. Finally he decided on a blue & maroon striped shirt, blue jeans & his bull hide boots. There, fit to ride or court or both, he thought as he looked in the mirror.

He stopped in the kitchen to talk to Maria. After telling Maria his plans for the afternoon and knowing the details would be handled, he sat down at the dining room table with a large glass of iced tea and the Sunday paper. Becca and Roy had decided to start around ten, so he had an hour before she was due downstairs. He probably should have awakened her but decided the extra sleep would do her good. Roy looked at his watch, 9:55. He thought about checking to see if Becca was up. Just as he stood to go upstairs Roy heard footsteps. He turned and looking him straight in his eyes was Becca. Roy's heart stopped, if she was beautiful last night, she was gorgeous today. Her red hair was swept back into a French braid, a green western shirt that was filled out in all the right places, blue jeans and boots. Staring was about all that he could do, his heart raced, his mouth went dry, he was afraid he would fall. Quickly, Becca grabbed his hands and gave him a quick kiss and led him toward the back door.

Hand in hand, they walked to the stable. Roy pushed open the stable doors, letting the midday light flood the stables. Roy walked down the aisle, petting the horses as he went. TomCat and Mr. Pay both nickered at him. Rubbing their noses, he passed them by and proceeded to the last two stalls.

"This is Hobie," Roy said pointing to a sorrel colored horse with a white spot just behind the left shoulder. "He is gentle and can go all day. Let me introduce you to the ranch's pride and joy. This is Star." The huge Palomino stallion stuck his head over the half door, the huge star in the middle of his forehead acted as a beacon, drawing Roy and Becca to look at him. Star was wound tighter than a seven-day clock this morning, his head was held high and fire gleamed from his eyes. Taking the lead rope off the nail, Roy snapped it on Star and led him out of the stall and over to the far side of the aisle, taking care to not get stepped on by his prancing hooves. After making sure that Star was fastened to the wall securely, Roy got Hobie out of his stall and clipped the gelding to the wall.

Walking over to the tack room, Roy handed a blanket and bridle to Becca, then he grabbed a saddle. Following Roy's instructions Becca laid the blanket over the sorrel's back. Roy tossed the saddle over his back and then tightened up the cinch. The bridle slipped easily over his head and Hobie stood quietly waiting on Star to be saddled. Surprisingly, Star stood fairly quiet as Roy saddled and put the headstall on.

"Let help me you up," he offered, holding the stirrup and offering Becca a knee to step on. Roy's head filled with excitement as Becca brushed up against him as she climbed aboard Hobie. Sensing his orneriness, Roy then led Star a safe distance away, grabbed a hunk of mane and stepped into the saddle. No sooner had he sat down than Star catapulted straight up in the air, head down and legs stiff, in an attempt to throw his rider. Roy worked over into a patch of tall grass next to the barn and just as quickly as it started it was over. Roy looked over at Becca's startled face and smiled.

"Sorry to scare you, he does it every time you first get on him, just to see who's boss," Roy commented matter-of-factly. "Are you ready to ride, Becca?"

"I am ready to ride, if you are done showing off, Mr. Curtis," Becca said curtly, but with a slight smile just to let him know that she was impressed.

"Then we are off, our adventure awaits." Reigning Star around and heading down the path, Becca nudged Hobie forward and soon they were riding side by side. For the next couple of hours they rode across the farm, talking about their lives, cooking chili, car races and just enjoying each other. They rode through a wooded area and smelled the scent of the trees, passed through the main pasture, where Roy pointed out to Becca certain cows and their calves. Reaching the gate to the back pasture Roy leaned over, opened the gate, and let Becca lead the way. Making sure the gate was shut Roy nudged Star forward and quickly caught up with Becca and the gelding. Coming up over a ridge, Roy pointed to a grove of cottonwood trees next to a large stream.

"That's our destination." Roy said as he prodded Star into a slow canter down the hill. The grove was about 50 square yards with long lush grass under the trees. Next to the stream there was a spot that looked a little out of place and Becca peered through the trees at a clearing that looked to have been mowed and trimmed.

Roy slid from his saddle, dropped reign and walked over to help Becca down. He placed his hands on each side of her waist and lifted her down. Standing face to face, Becca planted a quick kiss on his lips and then ran through the trees.

"What a great place for a picnic," Becca squealed with delight, spinning around and looking at everything at once. "Too bad we didn't bring one!!"

"Ask and you shall receive," Roy laughed, emerging from behind a tree carrying a small cooler and a couple of blankets. Spreading the blankets out on the short grass next to the stream, Roy motioned for Becca to join him. The cooler contained sandwiches, some salads, and drinks.

"How did you get this stuff here?" Becca asked as she finished off the last of the salad. "This food is great."

"My magnificent housekeeper made it and how it got here is magic," Roy smiled and reached over and lightly kissed her. Lying back on the blanket, Roy stretched out and looked up at the clouds. Becca lay against him and looked him in the eyes. Gently she kissed him. The sunlight encircled her face as Roy looked up at her; the scent of her perfume ignited a stirring deep inside of him. He pulled her close and kissed her, enjoying the feel of her body. Becca suddenly giggled, jumped up, and ran toward the stream.

Pulling off her boots, Becca waded into the water until it was up her knees. "Look familiar?" she called to Roy. "Of course I did have a formal on last time."

"Yeah and last time it took me a month to get my boots clean and dry."

"So what are you going to do?" Becca said teasingly, peeling off her shirt and throwing it onshore to reveal her bikini top.

Roy pulled his boots and socks off, and following Becca's lead, took off his shirt also. He slowly made his way to the river. Looking toward the stream he could see Becca playing in the water with the rivulets of water sliding delicately down her back. So absorbed was he in her body that almost too late did he spy the cottonmouth snake preparing to strike. Letting out a scream, Roy dove at Becca in an attempt to push her out of harm's way. Becca buckled as Roy's body plowed into her side, like a linebacker tackling a wide receiver. As they both hit the water, Roy felt the venomous fangs plunge deep into his right leg. Pain shot through the calf muscle as he yanked the snake away and crushed the snake's head against a rock. Quickly, he turned to look for Becca and found her standing in the middle of the stream. She just stood there staring at him with an ashen look on her face. Extending his hand, he helped Becca out of the river and to the blankets, covering her to keep her warm. Only then did he look down at his leg and examine the bite, two punctures an inch apart in the meat of his calf.

Already the leg was starting to ache and turn red. Roy looked at

Becca and with as much composure as he could muster, told her to get dressed quickly. With each movement, Roy could feel the poison work its way slowly up his leg toward his knee. Grabbing his kerchief he fashioned a tourniquet around his leg to slow the blood flow, but the adrenalin rush had moved it quickly through his body and he was beginning to feel weak. He looked over at Becca as she buttoned the last button on her blouse and headed towards the horses. Though white with the fear that Roy might not make it, Becca managed to unhobble the horses and led them over to Roy.

"We have to get you to a doctor, but it's a good two-hour ride back to the ranch house. Roy, can you make it?" Becca inquired gently holding his face between her hands. Roy's face was already sweating with a fever and he was starting to shake.

"There is a cell phone in my bag, you can call for help. If we follow the trail up over that ridge," Roy pointed up to the north, "we will come to the state highway. It will be a rough ride but I think I can make it if you lead and we hurry." Becca handed Roy his boots, but his right one would not go on as the swelling increased. When he stood up, Roy thought he was going to pass out the pain was so incredible. It felt as if hot oil was being poured down the inside of his leg, he leaned against Star's saddle until the rush subsided. With Becca's help, Roy managed to pull himself into the saddle and head out.

"Star, my friend, I need your help. Take me to the road." The big stallion sensing that his rider was hurt, walked with a slow, deliberate gait. Roy's body reeled with pain. Fearing he would fall off, Roy grabbed a pigging string and tied his hands to the horn to balance him. In his blurred state, all Roy could think about was what a lady he had found and if this was love then it was worth dying for, but living for it was even better.

"911, what is your emergency?" the operator said, once Becca was able to get a cell signal. It had taken her five tries to get through.

"Yes, my boyfriend has been bitten by a snake and is very sick," Becca said, her voice beginning to show the stress of the situation.

"Where are you located?" the operator asked.

"I am not sure. We were riding and I am new to the area."

"I have your phone's GPS location. Can your boyfriend be moved?"

"Yes, we are on horseback and headed toward a state highway."

"I have the ambulance dispatched and I am monitoring your location. Please keep your phone on to keep your GPS signal active." Slowly, they picked their way up the hill. Becca scrolled through the contacts on Roy's phone until she found Justin's number. Justin answered on the second ring. As calmly as she could, Becca explained what had transpired. Justin assured her that he would handle everything else and all that she needed to do was concentrate on getting Roy to the road. As they rode, Becca wondered if it was really Roy's face in the dream catcher. Would Roy make it? Would she ever hold him again? How selfless he had been when he dove to save her. Becca wept silently, not wanting Roy to hear.

Finally, they reached the fence line at the edge of the road, just a hundred yards down the line was a gate. The pair reached the gate just as the ambulance came into view. Becca was off of the gelding, tied him and then taking the reigns from Roy, led Star to the road. The medics carefully cut the string that held Roy on the Palomino and eased Roy down onto the stretcher. Henri and Maria arrived just as they were loading him into the ambulance. Henri took the horses from Becca and motioned for her to go. Maria crossed herself and told her that they would meet her at the hospital. Becca followed the medics into the back, they pulled the door shut and to the wail of the siren they headed for the hospital.

The medic turned and asked Becca, "You're his wife? Correct?"

With tears streaming from her eyes she said, "No, but I have to be with him. He saved my life and I just gotta to go with him to make sure that he will be alright."

"I am really not supposed to let you," the paramedic said.

"You must let me go, please," pleaded Becca. The medic looked at her carefully and figured that she would stay out of the way. Even though it was only eight miles to the hospital in Goshen, it seemed like eight hundred to Becca. The medic checked Roy's vital signs and then got on the radio and talked to the emergency room. He talked in low tones so Becca couldn't make out everything the medic was saying, but she could make out words like: "pulse thready, shocky, anaphylactic, and atropine." After the last word, the medic reached into the cabinet above the gurney and took a syringe of medicine and injected it into the IV that was running into Roy's arm. Checking his vital signs once again, the medic tapped on the door twice and Becca felt the ambulance surge forward. Becca reached up and touched Roy's hand and tears filled her eyes.

"Roy, you have to get better so that I can have that dance you promised me," Becca whispered to him.

The sirens and the lights were flashing and it seemed to take forever to get to the hospital but when they arrived, the doctor and trauma team on call were waiting as the doors opened. They all reached inside and within a second they had Roy out of the ambulance and were wheeling him into the hospital trauma room.

As the doors closed behind the last nurse, Becca ran to the door and tried to get in. A nurse came out and said, "I'm sorry but you will have to stay in the waiting room."

"Please let me know as soon as you can how he is doing, PLEASE," she said as she held the nurses hand, "and please tell him that I love him." Slowly she turned toward the waiting room. As she walked past the entrance, Justin, Lisa, Geoff and Halsey rushed in. Halsey wrapped her arms around Becca and along with Lisa led her to the waiting area. Geoff and Justin headed to the information desk to find out what was going on.

What little resolve Becca had left, dissolved into Halsey's arms. "I'm so sorry, it's my fault."

"No, it's not," Lisa said.

"Yes, it is," Becca sobbed. "We were laying there on the blankets and I got goofy and ran into the stream and tempted Roy to follow and now he is dying." The tears flowed freely out of Becca's eyes. Halsey held her tight, trying to calm her. Geoff and Justin walked in and paced back and forth, having received no further information from the front desk.

It seemed like hours before the nurse came out to waiting room. Walking across the room toward the five of them, she said, "Did you folks come in with Mr. Curtis?"

"Yes," Becca said, looking up at the nurse. "I rode in the ambulance here with him. Can I see him?"

"We are getting ready to move him to ICU, but you can go in and see him first. Before you do, please remember that he is very sick and may not be able to respond to you, also, please keep your visit short."

As Becca walked in she stopped and took a deep breath, Roy looked so helpless laying in the bed with all the tubes and things hooked up to him. She walked to the bed, slowly sat down next to him and touched his hand. It was cool, but she held it tightly and leaned into him gently, whispering as she did, "Roy, you have to get better, you promised me a dance and I don't want to miss it. Remember, baby."

She then kissed his face and wiped the tear that had fallen on his face. Sitting back down on the bed she watched him breathe. Looking up to heaven as if God was listening to her, she prayed.

"God I never have been good at this and I know that you take care of those that need it, and if you could find it in your heart please don't take him away from me." She sat still and watched him. Becca thought that she could feel his hand tighten.

"Roy, honey, can you hear me? You have to get well." As she leaned down and kissed him good-bye, the nurses and aides were there to move him. Reluctantly Becca returned to the waiting room, Lisa took her hand and they headed toward the elevator. They had just exited the elevator onto the intensive care unit floor, when a look of panic spread across Becca's face.

"I have to go to work tomorrow," Becca said, "but I need to stay here." Clearly not thinking straight, she put her hands on her head and tried to shake the thoughts into place.

"Easy, Becca," Lisa said, "Hals and I will take care of everything. Give me your work number." Without thinking, Becca rattled off Pam's cell and the office number. Lisa stayed with Becca as Halsey went down to make a couple of calls.

Doctor Levi Hostetler was perplexed. For thirty plus years he had practiced medicine and he had never seen a snake bite react the way this one had. Roy's leg was beet red and fifty percent larger than it should have been. The anti-venom had stabilized his vitals, but Roy was obviously in severe pain. Roy had screamed when Dr. Hostetler had touched his leg, so for the moment they kept him sedated. That it was a poisonous snakebite in the first place was strange. There were only about three types of poisonous snakes in Indiana and they lived way to the south. The fang marks on Curtis' leg verified it was a cottonmouth snake, and the anti-venom had worked. So what was causing the swelling and pain? He didn't have any definitive answers, but his friends needed to know that he was working on it.

"Geoff, Halsey." Doctor Hostetler addressed the Barrington's. He knew them and Roy Curtis from being on the lake together.

"Doc, this is Roy's friend, Becca Davidson, and his manager, Justin, and his wife Lisa." Geoff made the quick introductions.

"I would like to say it's a pleasure, but under the circumstances."

"What did you find out? How is he doing?" Justin interrupted.

"Well for one thing, it was a cottonmouth bite of some sort. Yes, I know it is too far north, but that is what the blood test confirmed. But he is still in a lot of pain, his leg is terribly swollen and I am not sure what is causing it so we are keeping him sedated," the doctor explained.

"Can I see him?" Becca asked, fearing the answer.

"Yes, you can see him. He isn't awake though."

"That's OK; I just need to be with him." Becca headed down to Roy's room. Roy's breathing was steady and the blip of the machine sounded healthy to Becca. Roy was red with fever and even sedated he tossed and turned with pain. Halsey and Geoff stopped in before they left and asked if she wanted to go get some fresh air. Becca politely declined. Pulling up the chair, she sat there holding his hand and wiping the feverish sweat from his brow.

About three hours later, Doctor Hostetler walked in the room and took a look at Curtis' chart. Becca went to leave, but the doctor motioned her to stay. As he wrote in the chart, he pulled up another chair and looked at Becca.

"I talked to Maria and she gave me the OK to tell you everything," Doc Hostetler began. "I don't know if you were aware but Henri and Maria are considered next of kin for medical purposes, so they have the say on Roy's treatment while he is sedated. Anyway, Roy has two problems; one is the bite poison, which fortunately the anti-venom is fighting successfully. Second is an infection in his blood, we are not sure what caused it or if it has been hiding in his system and the bite caused it to flare up. We are starting him on some really powerful antibiotics to fight the infection."

"Will he get better?" Becca asked.

"His chances are good, the next twenty four hours are critical. We will know better after that. Now may I suggest that you go and get some food and a little rest?"

"No thank you, I am going to stay here next to him." Sliding the big easy chair over beside the hospital bed, Becca began her vigil. Rising only to grab a bite to eat, and then only if someone else was there, Davidson watched the man that she had come to love, even though she had just met him a few months prior, lay there in pain as the antibiotics fought the poison that flowed through his body.

Becca hadn't realized the number of friends that Roy had until they came streaming to see him. Every day Becca met a new friend of Roy's. Geoff stopped in every day and Halsey brought Becca clean clothes. Pam had called and said not to worry about work and to stay as long as she needed. The room filled with cards and flowers.

On the seventh day, the fever broke and by the end of the day, Roy was sitting up, ready to eat. "Have you been here the whole time?" Curtis inquired. "You didn't need to, I would have been fine."

"I know I didn't have to, but I wasn't going to let them slip you out the back door or something without me knowing it."

"You do look pretty good sitting there," Roy commented as looked intently at her red hair.

Unsure if she could answer without crying, she let the compliment pass and changed the subject. "Dr Hostetler said that once the fever broke you should be able to go home within a couple of days. Now that you are awake I am going to slip back to the farm and change clothes, OK? Bye, Roy. I'll be back."

With that, she rose, leaned over and kissed Roy softly on the lips, lingering for just a moment, her hands holding on to his, she looked him directly in eyes and smiled. "I am so happy you're going to be alright. I don't think I could have dealt with that."

"Hurry back," Roy said. "I kind of like it when you're near." As he finished that final comment Becca slipped out the door and headed back to the ranch.

Doctor Hostetler walked in for evening rounds and was glad to see Roy awake. "Where is your girlfriend?" he asked Roy as he checked his leg.

"She went to shower and change clothes," Roy said and added with a smile. "I suspect she'll be back soon."

"You do know she sat here all week with you," Doc commented. "A keeper if you ask me."

"I was thinking of keeping her, a pretty good filly with a lot of staying power."

"Think you can handle such a high-spirited filly?"

"Yeah, I sure hope so," was all Roy could think to say.

It took a couple more days for the swelling in Roy's leg to diminish to the point that Dr. Hostetler felt comfortable sending him home. Becca spent every spare minute with him, talking and getting to know him better. Finally, ten days after the bite, Becca rolled the wheelchair to the hospital door and loaded Roy into the truck and headed for the farm.

Maria had set up a hospital-style bed in the media room for Roy to stay in. The doctor had instructed Roy to keep his leg elevated and neither Maria nor Becca would let him ignore those orders. Roy was still really weak from his ordeal and it took real effort to climb the stairs to his room. He had been home a week when Dave Mitchell called and suggested dinner at the Barbee Hotel.

"Sure," Roy agreed, "I am getting a bad case of cabin fever so a little fresh air will do me good. Besides Becca is leaving Sunday and it would be great to look at her sitting somewhere other than next to this bed." Roy shared the plans with Becca and headed slowly up the stairs. He had been upstairs about twenty minutes when Becca heard the sound of something hitting the wall and the glass breaking. Fearing Roy had fallen, she raced up the stairs. Becca entered Roy's room to find him sitting with his head in his hands. One boot was on; the other was lying against the wall, a broken vase underneath it.

"I can't go," Roy sobbed. "They don't fit, I can't get it on."

"It's OK," Becca tried to comfort him.

"No it's not. What do you think I am going to wear. These?" Roy held up a pair of black tennis shoes. The kind of shoes with Velcro straps that elderly men in nursing homes wore was what Roy wanted to say.

"No, you don't have to wear those. Change out of your jeans and into a pair of khakis and put on these." Becca handed him his white cross-trainers. "Now hurry, Dave and Sara are on their way and you owe me a couple of dances." With that she left the room.

# Chapter 14

It took two months for Roy to completely recover from the snakebite incident. Becca came over every weekend to visit and help Roy deal with mood swings and depression. During one of the up swings, Becca finally got the courage to ask about Jacki and Brent. At first Roy became sullen and refused to talk, but Becca pushed the point.

"Look, Roy, I am not trying to replace or compete with her, I just want to know about the lady you loved. From what Lisa and Halsey tell me, we probably could have been best friends."

"OK," Roy finally relented. "I met Jacki, my junior year at Ohio State University. She was walking across campus with a bunch of her girlfriends. I just waded into the middle of them and introduced myself."

"Sounds familiar," Becca interjected. "I guess I am not the first lady you waded in after."

"I guess not," Roy chuckled at the similarities. "Anyway two years later we were married."

For the next two hours Roy talked about Jacki and Brent, even reliving the night they were killed and the pain that had existed ever since. That was until last June, when he waded in after another woman. By the end of the evening, Roy was crying, but the memory of them was sweeter and he felt better than he had ever felt about that night. Somehow he could go on with life and this lady just might be the one to ride the river with.

Roy's recovery came steadily after that night. The swelling decreased noticeably each day. In Roy's mind, his recovery was finished the morning he finally could pull on his work boots and head for the barn.

Becca had spent just about every hour at the hospital those first few days and had treated him to a romantic evening at the farm the Friday after he got home as her way of saying thanks. This statuesque redhead occupied his mind every free minute and some of time when he should have been concentrating on something else. This daydreaming had led him into his current predicament.

It was fall roundup time on the ranch and they had been bringing in the herd from the south section pasture all week. Since the crew worked every hour of daylight and slept in the line shack, Roy had not seen or talked to Becca since late Sunday evening. The roundup had gone smoothly and it looked like they would be done before the evening. This would allow for a much-needed break until Monday. Curtis was pushing the last of the cows and calves towards the pens when his mind began to drift to that night he had met Becca Davidson and the way time had almost stopped as they sat on the dock.

"Hey, watch out!" Matt, one of the hands hollered. "They are going to cut back!" Ordinarily, Roy would have seen the old boss cow lift her head and have cut her off before she could break with the herd. Swinging Star hard to the left, he tried to block the cow's escape route, but she had the jump she needed and took off for the high country. Her lead was followed by about two dozen other cows and calves that darted through the hole created by the cut to the left. With her head up and obviously pleased with herself the old cow led the bunch of renegades up over the hill to the high country.

Mad at himself for not paying attention, Curtis wheeled his horse around to stop the rest of the cattle from getting away. Quickly he and the other hands finished pushing the cows into the outer pens. As the gates closed, he looked off to the south to see the small herd topping the hill. *Oh well, at least the other three hundred are in the pen.* The way he figured it, if he would have tried to stop them the whole herd would have split and they would have had to chase everything again. This way just one person's, daydreamer Curtis', weekend would be screwed up chasing his two dozen ornery cows.

Shaking his head, Roy rode over to the horse corral to get a fresh mount. Star was an excellent workhorse and could go all day long, but it had been a rough week and Curtis was going to need all the speed and agility to move these cows back home. Roy slid down off of the Palomino and handed the reins to Miguel and went to get something to drink.

"Probably better saddle up Mr. Pay for me," Roy told Miguel as he opened the cooler for a can of Mt. Dew, "and get on the radio and see if Chris is done with Roscoe and Barney. If he is, have him bring them over." Mr. Pay was the black Appaloosa that could cut cows with the best of them. Matt liked to say that he could turn on a dime and leave nine cents change. Aside from Star he was Roy's favorite horse, but you needed to stay awake when you rode him because he would leave you sitting astride air when he turned. Roscoe and Barney were the Seven C Cattle Company's two cattle dogs. Both full-blooded Australian Shepherds, the dogs could root cows out of the brush better than any horse. Curtis didn't think that a better combination existed than the two dogs and Mr. Pay. Because of their ability, Roy would often send the two dogs out with one of hands to move the cattle from one pasture to another.

Curtis finished his drink and had eaten a sandwich by the time Chris's F250 rolled up to the line shack. Chris Freeman, a tall lanky young man, served as the herdsman for the registered cowherd and had been with the Seven C for almost five years.

"Hey, boss! I hear you're sleeping in the saddle again," Freeman teased as he let the dogs out of the back of the truck. "I guess Miss

Becca ain't gonna see her man tonight."

"Aw shut up!" Roy fired back, throwing his empty pop can at Chris. Curtis had been single and alone for so long that he blushed like a schoolboy at the mention of his new love. "Come on dogs, let's get out of here before the rest of the pack circles in for the kill. Have a great weekend my friends." With that final word, Curtis grabbed a hunk of mane, slid his boot into the stirrup, stepped up into the saddle and headed off after the strays.

The southern range was rolling pasture with large gullies and ravines throughout. Roy knew it was a fifty-fifty chance that he would find the cows before dark and get them pointed back towards home. So here he was out in the hills trying to find a small herd of cows that didn't want to be found, when he should have been heading to Becca's for dinner. He hoped that she got the message that he had to hastily leave on her machine from the truck's cell phone just before he left.

He had never felt so in love with a person as he did with Becca. Her long red hair and blue eyes captivated his very soul. She looked absolutely great in jeans or a dress. He hoped that the passion between them would never die.

Just then Roscoe let out a yip and took off for a pile of brush about 150 yards away with Barney right behind him going flat out. Jerked back to reality for the second time today, Roy sank his spurs into Mr. Pay's flanks and took off after the dogs. Circling to the south Curtis arrived just as the dogs herded the cows and calves out of the tangle. The dogs worked quickly and soon the animals were headed north toward the corrals. Roy pointed Mr. Pay into the center and put the dogs on each flank. Pushing the small herd hard the dogs and rider kept cows heading down the trail. Every once in a while the old boss cow would start to wander left or right, but a quick whistle to Roscoe or Barney and the dogs would push her back to trail.

Three hours after they had taken off for the hills, the herd of cows passed through the gates to the outer corrals. Curtis looked at his watch, it read eight p.m. If he hurried he could be at the house in half an hour, shower and be on his way to Becca's house by nine.

"Come on, guys, let's go." At a full gallop, Roy flew down the lane the mile to the house with the dogs running right beside him. Maybe, just maybe, Becca wouldn't be too mad.

# Chapter 15

It was late December, the university was on Christmas break and Becca was spending the weekend at the farm, something she had been doing more and more of since Roy had been bitten in August. Roy had promised a great weekend of open houses and parties. Since school was on break, she had packed her best and driven there just as it began to snow.

The snow had been falling steadily for the last four hours and almost six inches of the fluffy white stuff covered the ground. It was a perfect snow; big fat flakes coming straight down like a scene from *White Christmas*. Becca pulled the dark green turtleneck sweater over her head and looked out the window one more time. Roy had called in from the barn and told her to dress nicely, but very warmly, and he would be up to pick her up in about fifteen minutes. So she had quickly changed from her robe to a pair of jeans and the sweater. Becca had just finished pulling on her winter boots when she heard what sounded like a cowbell outside the back door. Grabbing her thick down coat and gloves, she hurried down to the back door.

"Your carriage awaits, madam." Roy greeted her as she opened the door. Stepping aside and with a sweep of his Stetson, Roy showed her the sleigh. The cutter was a highly polished dark green with gold pinstripes. Pulling the cutter was a matched team of chestnut colored geldings, complete with bells on the black harness.

"Oh, Roy, it is beautiful." Becca ran through the snow to the old sleigh and ran her long fingers across the polished wood. "Where'd you get it?"

"It was my grandfather's and we just finished the restoration work on it last week. Justin and I have been working on it for the last year."

"You did an excellent job, and the horses are just grand looking."

"Thank you. Do you want to take a ride?"

"I thought you would never ask," Becca replied, taking Roy's extended hand as he helped her into the sleigh. The seat was upholstered with heavy, plaid wool and would have originally been stuffed with a coarse fill. Roy had instead sent the seat section to a friend who ran an upholstery shop and had the seat covered with the same material used in the seat of some of the finest cars in the world. As Becca settled into the seat a blast of cold wind hit her face.

"I don't mean to be a party pooper, but does this thing have a heater?" she inquired as a shiver raced down her back.

"Ask and you shall receive." Curtis produced a small chemical activated heater to set at her feet. "And now something to help keep the heat in, a genuine buffalo blanket." Roy produced a large, luxurious blanket made out of the cape of the American bison. The weight of it ensured Becca that the heat would not escape and that the wind would not penetrate. Roy walked around to the other side, climbed in and tucked the huge blanket around his lap.

"Ready?" he asked

"Ready."

"Then hold on. Giddy up!" Roy grabbed the buggy whip out of the holder and gave it a crack above the haunches of the two horses. The pair shot forward; Becca was glad that she was hanging on as she rocked against the back of the sleigh. The team accelerated to a fast trot and headed effortlessly down the lane. Roy turned the rig down the lane that headed to the back of the farm and eased the team down to a fast walk.

"Casey and Ted will need their speed later," Roy said, referring to the horses. "Comfortable?"

"Yeah." Becca cuddled against Roy. He pulled her close and wrapped his arm around her. For the next ten minutes they enjoyed the ride and each other. The sun was setting and the sky had a golden cast to it as the last rays of daylight reflected off of the fresh snow. The wind picked up a little and Becca understood the line from the old song, *"stings the toes & bites the nose."* She didn't care and just snuggled a little closer to Roy. As they reached the end of the back lane Becca figured that it would be time to turn around, for the county surely would have plowed the road that ran along the back of the farm. Instead of slowing to turn around, Roy swung the cutter out onto an unplowed road.

"The owners along this stretch of road decided that they needed a place to use their sleighs so we convinced the county to close off the road and not to plow it in the winter. We take turns packing it down until it is as smooth as glass," Roy explained. "This nine mile stretch of road is home to some of the best cutters in the county, take a look ahead."

Becca could see a large ornate sleigh with ten to twelve people on it, being pulled by four huge draft horses. As they pulled up alongside of it, Becca recognized some of the people from the parties she had attended with Roy. Driving the big rig was an elderly man and his wife. The passengers varied in age from preschoolers to senior citizens.

"Hey, Jim. You wanna race?" Roy challenged good-naturedly.

"Well, Roy, it's like this," Jim hollered back. "Shirley wouldn't be able to invite you over again if I beat you. Some other time."

"OK, see you at the Millers." And with a light tap of the whip, he surged past the big sleigh and down the road. The Millers were a Mennonite family that lived about four miles down the road and in twenty minutes he turned the rig into the back drive. Pulling up to the house, a young man grabbed Casey's halter until they got out and led the team over with the others. Becca turned to grab the blanket to take it in the house, but Roy stopped her.

"The blankets will be put in the tack room and kept warm," Roy told Becca. "Now let's go in the house and do the same." The farmhouse was like so many in the area, big and white. Helen Miller opened the door and gave Roy a big motherly hug and then took Becca by the hands and welcomed her.

"It is so good to finally meet you, I have heard so much about you." This comment rated a look from Becca to Roy who could only shrug his shoulders in reply. Taking their coats, Helen led them to the living room where the women were gathered. Leaving Becca with Sara Mitchell, he headed to the dining room where the real business was being conducted.

"What is going on?" Becca asked Sara.

"Oh, Roy didn't tell you?" Sara asked. "It's sleigh races tonight at midnight."

"Really? Sounds like fun, but it is so cold outside."

"You think so?" Lisa Roberts said as she entered the room carrying a couple of mugs of hot-spiced cider. "Wait till you're doing break neck and hell bent on the back road. That is cold. Here you are going to need this."

"Thanks." Becca sipped the cider and nearly choked as the cognac-laced cider burned her throat. "With this I might get cold but I wouldn't care."

"Exactly," Sara said and everyone laughed. For the next three hours they ate snacks and sipped cider; the men stayed in the dining room and haggled about horses and starting spots.

"It's time to bundle up and keep the men from killing themselves," Helen said, passing out the coats.

The night scene was absolutely beautiful when they walked out of the house. The large moon cast its glow onto the snow-covered landscape. Just a few snowflakes were still falling adding to the wonderland feel. Becca grabbed Roy's arm with both of hers and walked to their cutter. True to his word, the blanket was warm and the heater on.

"This is how it works," Roy explained. "Each type of rig is given a handicap in minutes based on size and speed. The cutter drew a zero.

That means everybody scores based on my time. There are five heats and we will finish at the Franklin's for breakfast at five a.m."

"Five in the morning? You mean all night long?" Becca asked incredulously.

"Well yeah, we can sleep all day tomorrow. We will take appropriate breaks for cider." Roy smiled as he looked at her.

For the next five hours, twenty sleighs raced up and down the nine-mile stretch of road, bells jingling, noses cold and toes frozen. Everyone had a great time, after the third race, Helen had warm pie ready to eat. With their stomachs filled they were off again. By the fifth race everyone was ready to quit and it was a fast race to the Franklin's. Becca almost swooned when she smelled the fragrances coming from the kitchen. Ham and eggs were served in generous portions followed by waffles, biscuits and sausage gravy. The men ate as if they had been on a forty-day fast. Roy was keeping up with the rest, eating a dozen eggs and six slices of ham. The three waffles covered with apples more than filled Becca's appetite. While they were partaking in the feast, Sam Franklin stood to announce the winners.

"In first place is Dave Mitchell with nine hundred seventy points. Second is Roy Curtis with nine hundred twenty." Sam handed each of them an envelope filled with prize money.

"Who is last?" someone hollered.

"In last place and fixing breakfast for the next race is…. Drum roll, please." Sam allowed the proper pregnant pause before announcing the loser, "Mike 'The Slow Poke' Williams." Everyone cheered and laughed.

At six-thirty Roy and Becca said their goodbyes and began the sleigh ride home. The pace home was much slower as Casey and Ted were as tired as their passengers. Becca once again snuggled against Roy's large shoulder. The soft jingle of the bells and steady clip clop of the team's hooves lulled Becca to sleep. Roy held her tightly until he pulled up to his house. Miguel was waiting to take the horses. Roy gently woke Becca and together the walked to the house. Taking her up the stairs, kissed her good morning, and sent her to bed.

The winter semester was going great; Becca and Pam were booked solid with presentations. Their reputations had continued to grow and just about every elementary within driving distance of Moluntha State University had called and tried to schedule them. The main reason was that the pair were very good instructors but in part because the session on the Native Americans fulfilled the state's new history requirements. It came as a surprise to both of the women when Dr. Houchin announced the program change at the monthly staff meeting.

"Ms. Davidson and Ms. Gibson," Dr. Houchin began. "I have scheduled you two ladies to go to Canada for three weeks in March. There is a Native American conference in Winnipeg that we want you to attend and then you will be doing some research on the Canadian Tribes."

"What about our teaching sessions?" Becca asked.

"I have thought about that and had Sharon reschedule the month of March."

"OK, what will we be doing with the research?" Pam inquired.

"The Academic Division wants the department to expand the American Studies and your research will be the foundation of the expansion," Dr. Houchin said. "You will leave on March fifth and return March twenty-sixth; you will present your findings at the April department meeting. Since you will be going from one remote area to another I have arranged for charter air service for the trip. Sharon will have your itineraries ready by tomorrow afternoon. One other thing…dress warmly."

"Thank you for the reminder," Becca said with as much sarcasm as she thought she could get away with, so much for spending spring break in the tropics with Roy. The meeting lasted another twenty minutes before breaking up. Pam and Becca headed back to their offices with mixture of feelings ranging from disappointment to excitement.

"Stink," Becca muttered as they walked into their office. "Roy's going to be out of town until after we leave."

"That's right. He's in south Texas, isn't he?"

"Yeah, he is working on a deal with some big ag conglomerate. He isn't supposed to be back until spring break," Becca said.

"Well, I guess Chris and Roy will be spending break together," Pam noticed. "I guess we had better make a couple of calls."

"Good evening, darling," Roy answered his cell phone on the second ring, caller ID letting him know that Becca was calling. "Wassup? Miss me?"

"You know I how much I miss you," Becca said. "I have some not-so-good news."

"What's wrong?" Roy said, sitting up on the edge of the hotel bed where he had been watching TV.

"Pam and I are going to Winnipeg." Becca told him about the conference and the research trip.

"I guess no Marsh Islands this year," Roy said, sounding just slightly disappointed.

"Roy, I am so sorry," Becca said almost crying.

"Hey, no crying now," Roy said, trying to sound cheery. "If we can't do the Bahamas in March, then we will do the Maldives in May. I promise."

"OK. I miss you so much."

"I miss you too. When we both get back we will spend a long weekend at the farm," Roy said. "Just be careful and dress warmly."

"Thanks for the reminder. I love you. Bye," Becca said.

"Bye, miss you," Roy said, flipping his phone shut. As he rolled on his back and stared at the hotel room ceiling, an uneasy feeling swept over him.

# Chapter 16

It was midnight and Becca finally had her suitcase packed. She had postponed packing it, choosing instead to spend the evening talking to Roy on the phone. Like a teenager, Becca had been curled up on the couch and had giggled and laughed with Roy, both not wanting to say good bye. Finally, Roy had said his goodbyes and hung up, leaving her to pack. After she had packed, Becca fixed a cup of tea and sat back on the couch listening to the smooth jazz tunes that floated from the stereo. She sat there thinking about how her life had changed in the last year. Last school year she was just a lonely wrench turner. Now she had a great job with a university and a man she loved. Absentmindedly, she looked up at the dreamcatcher; suddenly the image began to appear. This time it didn't fade away, but continued to come into focus. A smile broke across Becca's face as she recognized the roguish smile and bright eyes, they could only belong to the man she loved.

The King Air A100 turboprop jet was sitting on the tarmac when Becca and Pam pulled up to the Twin Eagle Air Charter service terminal. They would clear customs when they landed in Winnipeg, so the customer service representative took their bags and loaded them directly onto the plane. Pam and Becca took facing seats and buckled in for takeoff as the door was shut. The big Pratt & Whitney turboprop engines spun to life and the plane taxied from the terminal to the runway. The engines were at takeoff speed and the pilot released the brake sending the jet roaring down the runway.

Once in the air, Pam opened up the refreshment cooler and took out a couple of drinks. Becca set up her laptop and began to work; Pam sipped on her drink and took the opportunity to catch up on her reading. The four hour flight was very relaxing and set the tone for the rest of the trip. They cleared customs in Winnipeg easily and picked up their rental car. The conference didn't start until tomorrow so the ladies checked into their hotel, changed into their swimsuits and hit the hot tub. The afternoon was spent between the pool and hot tub talking about Roy and Chris and the directions their lives were going.

Roy was antsy to say the least. He missed Becca and it showed. He was short with his staff and a couple of times Mrs. Peterson had to politely calm him down. Even though they talked every evening and e-mailed daily love notes to each other, Roy couldn't get the nagging feeling of impending doom out of his mind. It was halfway through this three week trip that he decided that he couldn't survive without her and as soon as she got back he was going to ask her to marry him. Roy knew just how and where he was going to do it. Picking up the phone, he called Jessica Kilkenny and laid out his plans.

Becca flipped her cell phone shut in mild disgust, she had tried since they had arrived in this little town to get through to Roy, but either just got his, "You know what to do, leave a message," voicemail or no signal at all. The little hotel didn't have Internet, so she hadn't gotten any e-mails either. She couldn't believe how much she missed his voice and his big arms around her. Well, she would be at his place in four hours and then everything would be fine. Becca put on her blue down coat that Roy had bought her, picked up her luggage and headed for the door. Pam was exiting her room as Becca left hers so they headed for the car.

The cold arctic wind whipped hard around the corner of the small motel as Becca and Pam headed for their rental car. This was the last day of their research trip and though it had been a profitable three weeks interviewing different tribal elders about their tribe's history, they were glad to head home. When they had first arrived in Winnipeg, the weather had been a tolerable twenty degrees, but since they had headed east into the wilderness the temperatures had steadily dropped until the thermometer read a minus fifteen this morning with a chill factor of minus thirty-five degrees. Quickly the ladies loaded the last of their gear into the trunk and hopped into the frozen car. The cold engine groaned in protest but sputtered and started. Pam let it idle and warm up while they scraped ice off of the windows. Fortunately it was only a ten-minute drive from the hotel to the airport terminal, even with so short of a trip, they both felt like they were frozen stiff. Grabbing their bags, they ran as fast as they could into the terminal.

"Good morning, ladies," the counter agent greeted them. "You're flying with Twin Eagle Air?"

"Yes, we are," Pam answered, wondering why he asked since they were the only two people in the terminal. Her question was answered shortly.

"There will be a short delay; the ground crew is having trouble getting the plane de-iced." The agent pointed over to a counter with a large coffee pot and said. "Help yourself to some coffee and doughnuts while you wait."

"Hot coffee, great!" Becca exclaimed as she headed to the counter. "The plane isn't the only thing having trouble de-icing this morning." She poured two large cups, handing one to Pam. They sat down in a couple of overstuffed chairs and tried to get warm.

Roy thought today would never get here; he could not believe how long the last three weeks had seemed; the last couple of days had been even longer, because Becca had not been able to communicate due to her remote location. The flight that Becca and her assistant had chartered was due in at Midway around five in the afternoon; so only ten more hours. Not varying his morning routine, Roy showered and dressed. He knew that Becca liked him looking, as she called it, "dapper" rather than "banker boring," so in addition to his normal black suit he put on a royal blue paisley vest. Grabbing his mug of iced tea and his briefcase, Roy headed for the garage.

His blue BMW convertible roared to life as he turned the key. The sleek sports car shot out of the parking garage and onto the street, its tires squealing in protest as it slid into the morning rush. Not one to normally drive like a mad man, but the thought of Becca coming home just seemed to fire him up. He hoped that he wasn't reading more into this relationship than he should, but there always seemed to be a oneness between them from the beginning. Roy pondered over these thoughts as he worked his way through traffic to the office. Pulling into his reserved parking spot, Roy looked at his watch and thought, *Only nine and one half more hours.*

"Good morning, Helen," Roy greeted as he headed for his office. "I know that I have a meeting with the Parkers about the Farmers Elevator acquisition at one, but is there anything else pending?"

"No, Mr. Curtis, Mike Faraday called and set up an appointment for Monday morning at 10:00 a.m." Helen responded.

"Excellent, I need to be out of here by four, so I can be at Midway before five. We are due at the Kilkenny's tonight for dinner at seven."

"OK. I'll make sure you're out the door in plenty of time. Oh, that's right, Becca is due in today." Helen smiled. She was glad that Roy Curtis had finally found love. "Shall I order roses for you to take?"

"No, I don't need roses. On second thought, that is a wonderful idea, please do."

"Consider it done," Helen said, picking up the telephone to order them delivered.

The morning passed slowly; all Roy could think about was Becca and how much he had missed her over the last three weeks. He missed her touch, her laugh, her smile, her smell, he had not thought about those things since he had dated his late wife, Jacki, back in college.

"Hey, loverboy, you want to go get some lunch?" Mike Sheridan hollered through the door.

"Sure, we have a one o'clock so it will have to be quick."

"McMurphy's then?"

"McMurphy's it is."

The junior partners of Lescowitch, Meier, Curtis and Sheridan headed out the door and around the corner to McMurphy's Bar & Grill. They both ordered the lunch special of catfish and fries. Mike ordered a beer, but Mike drank too much and partied too much. Roy liked him any way; he was great at financial projections and analyzing statements and for that reason his partying was tolerated by the senior partners of the firm.

"So, Becca's coming home today," Mike said between sips of beer. "I bet you're happy."

"How did you know she was coming home?"

"It was easy, big boy. For the last three weeks you have been moping around the office like a lost puppy and today you can't sit still."

"Was it that obvious?"

"It couldn't have been more obvious if you had taken out a full page ad in the *Tribune*. So when are you going to pop the question?"

"What question?" Roy asked with a big grin. "Oh you mean asking her to marry me? I don't know, I was kind of thinking tonight at the Kilkenny's, but it is none of your business."

"Not a little scared are you?"

"Am not, just cautious."

"To quote a certain friend, whose initials are RC; if you are cautious, you're scared."

"Touché."

Fortunately for Roy their lunch came about that time and they could concentrate on eating and business. As they ate the two of them discussed strategy in the buy out of the Farmer's Elevator by the Parkers. Roy finished his iced tea and paid the bill. They had just enough time to get back to the office before the Parkers got there. Roy knew that Mrs. Peterson would have the conference room set up and ready to go, because she always did.

They were about halfway back to the office when a funny feeling came over Roy. Stopping he felt as though someone was calling to him in pain, but he couldn't place the voice that rattled inside his head.

"What's wrong?" Mike asked, looking at Roy as he just stood there on the sidewalk. "You don't look so good. Is everything OK?"

"Just had a funny feeling, not funny ha-ha, but funny as in strange. I could have sworn I heard someone screaming in fear, but for the life of me, I can't place the voice."

"Probably the catfish," Mike joked. "Anyway, we need to get back to the office for your one o'clock meeting."

"Yeah, you're probably right, let's go," Roy muttered, not totally convinced that Sheridan was right.

The Parkers were already in the conference room when they arrived back at the office. Roy couldn't shake that feeling of fear and knew he needed to do something about it. On his way to the conference room, he stopped by Mrs. Peterson's desk and spoke to her about it.

"I know it sounds strange," Roy continued after he had relayed the story to her, "but I feel like someone is trying to call to me. Will you humor me and call the charter service out at Midway and see if they have heard from Becca's flight. The charter service is called Twin Eagle Air Service. Let me know if you find out anything."

"I will call right away, Mr. Curtis. Do you want me to interrupt the meeting when I find out?"

"No, I need to put this deal to bed, so no phone calls or interruptions. Thanks."

"You're welcome, Mr. Curtis." Helen replied as she picked up the phone book to look for the number.

Roy shook hands with Bill and Ben Parker as he sat down at the table. Sheridan joined them shortly, bringing with him the final projections and financing arrangements for the acquisition. After Ben had a chance to review the changes he looked at Bill and simply nodded.

"Gentlemen," Ben Parker began, "I have spent my life in agribusiness and I believe that these are some of the best financing plans

I have ever seen. The question is can we sell it to the stockholders of the Farmer's Elevator? To answer my own question, yes, I think we can if we change just a couple of items." Ben turned his copy of the projections around so that Curtis and Sheridan could see the changes to the projections. He was about a third of the way through the first page when there was a knock on the door.

"Come in," Curtis snapped. How come every time he was in an important meeting someone had to bother him? Very slowly the door opened and Mrs. Peterson entered. From the look on her face, Roy knew that something was wrong. His fears were amplified when she motioned for him to come outside the conference room. Quickly, Helen led him to his office and shut the door.

"Mr. Curtis, I have some bad news and I think you'd better have a seat," Helen began. Curtis sat down in one of the chairs in front of his desk and looked at Mrs. Peterson. "I just got off the phone with the charter service, Mr. Curtis, and they say the plane is an hour overdue into Duluth from Canada, and they are afraid it might have gone down just inside the United States border."

The words drained the life from Roy's body and he slumped down in the chair. It couldn't be true, not again. He couldn't bear to lose someone to an accident for the second time. His head began to spin and his breathing became shallow and rapid. He could not believe what he was hearing, but the pain began deep within him and continued to grow.

"NOOOOO!!!!!" Roy wailed finally as the shock of what might be hit him. Never had anyone screamed in agony any louder or longer. Throughout the office every partner and secretary heard the cry and knew something was dreadfully wrong. The pain tore at the very essence of his soul and all the big man could do was sit and sob. When the tears could come no more and he was hoarse from crying, Roy put his face in his hands and rocked like a little child.

"Roy," Helen said when he had finally cried himself out, "I am not trying to offer false hope or anything of the sort, but the charter service only said the plane was past due and that they hadn't heard from it in over an hour. Let me get back on the phone to them and see if they have heard anything new."

Her words were like a cold splash of water on a hot summer day and they brought Roy back to reality. Somehow he knew she was still alive, though maybe hurt. The rational part of Curtis' being took over and he was suddenly thinking in the logic of the Marine Corps Lt. Colonel that he was. He knew that a telephone call would not satisfy him and that the only way would be to talk to the charter company face to face.

"Mrs. Peterson, I am going out to Midway to see what is going on personally," Roy said with a finality that even Mrs. Peterson would not argue with. "I will stop at the apartment and get some things first. If I have to, I'll catch a flight to Duluth and find out first-hand what happened." Curtis stood up and started to walk to the door, but his legs wobbled and he grabbed the arm of the chair for support.

"Mr. Curtis, are you sure you are fit to go?" Helen asked. "I would hate for you to hurt yourself before you found out about Becca."

"Yes, I am fine, Mrs. Peterson. Now I must be going."

Roy was about five steps from the door when Paul intercepted him. He made no attempt to stop Roy but rather fell in step beside him and walked with him to the garage. Neither said a word until they entered the building's parking garage, Roy shivered as they walked in to the cavernous space. The air was no longer brisk and refreshing to him, rather the cold cut to the bone. Paul placed his hand on Roy's shoulder and stopped him.

"Roy, I am not going to attempt to tell you that everything is going to be OK, because you and I both know how bad it could be." Paul paused for a moment to collect his thoughts. "What I guess I am trying to say is that we are here for you. Feel free to take all the time you need and use any of the firm's assets. Meier and Sheridan will cover your clients so don't worry about that. If you need anything let me know, OK?"

"Thanks, Paul. I'll let you know as soon as I find out. Right now I just have to get to the airport." Roy headed for the car; suddenly he stopped and turned around. "Hey Paul, could you ask Mrs. Peterson to call John Kilkenny and tell him I won't be able to be there for dinner. His work number is in my Rolodex. Thanks. Oh and somebody had better call the University and Pam Gibson's boyfriend also."

"I will take care of it myself. Now get," Paul answered.

With that Roy took off at a fast trot for his car. The sports car leapt out of the garage and headed for little Italy, he drove as fast as he dared, not wanting to risk a ticket. The car slid to a stop in front of the building and Curtis ran inside. Once inside his apartment, he grabbed his large duffle bag and tossed some cold weather gear in it, just in case. Picking up his personal phonebook he headed back out the door. The cold once again cut through his body and into his soul. Driving the car as if he were a Grand Prix driver, he raced for the airport. Traffic was light in the early afternoon and within thirty minutes he pulled up in front of the Twin Eagle Air Service office. Roy threw the office door open and headed for the sales counter. He hadn't taken three steps inside the door when a voice from the waiting area stopped him.

"Hey, Marine, don't you know you are out of uniform to go on a mission?" a voice inquired. Startled, Curtis stopped and spun around. In doing so, Roy came face-to-face with four men in winter gear and all bearing the eagle, globe and anchor insignia of the United States Marine Corps. Instantly a huge smile spread across Curtis' face and then a look of puzzlement at the sight of his commanding officer and friend Colonel Kilkenny.

"Good afternoon, sir. What are you doing here?" Roy asked.

"When your boss called and said that you would not be coming for supper and then told me why, I figured you might need a little support," Col. Kilkenny began. "As I headed out of the office at a near dead run, the First Sergeant here reminded me that two officers running around the back country alone would not be wise, so he made a telephone call and grabbed the gunny and we headed out. But the gunny didn't drive us here, but to the helipad where the warrant officer was waiting with the chopper blades spinning. So in we climb, and away we go."

First Sergeant Holycross interrupted. "I took one look at the CO's face after we lifted off and I know he is trying to figure out what he is going to tell HQ about us using Corps assets for personal use. So I looked at him and grinned, I told him not to worry because this is a squad level search and rescue emergency readiness exercise. We had Cold Blitz on the books but had not executed it. I kind of left it unused in case of a crisis. I sorta thought this qualified as one."

"Thanks, guys, for the thought, but I need to talk to the charter service."

"Sir," Murphy said, "the Colonel already spoke with the charter people and we know everything that they do. The gunner has the chopper ready and waiting. We will brief you in the air."

"Now, like I said earlier," Kilkenny spoke with command authority, "you are out of uniform, now go get out of that dandy gentleman's outfit and into uniform. Catch." John tossed a duffle at Curtis, which he caught one-handed and Gunnery Sergeant Washington handed Roy his personal one out of the car.

"Aye, Aye, sir." Curtis replied, did a crisp about face and headed to the men's room to change. Between the two bags there was enough cold weather gear to keep an Eskimo sweating. Hurriedly, Roy slipped out of his banker clothes and into his gear. Choosing the lighter-weight clothing so he could dress in layers, Curtis slipped on the silk long underwear and socks. Two layers of cotton and wool sweats and he was ready for the outer garments. Insulated boots, bibs, gloves and mittens were put on, followed by his USMC parka. He felt and looked somewhat like a polar bear as he left the restroom and entered the lobby.

The rest of the squad was waiting for him by the door. The five of them had served together in the Gulf and each knew the other's strengths and weaknesses. *A great group of men to ride the river with or to search for a lost plane* Roy thought.

The gunner had the chopper blades spinning hard as the other four Marines settled into their seats and shut the door. Roy pulled his headset on so he could talk to the others. The helicopter lifted off and headed at full speed to the north. Curtis was glad he had taken time to change into his winter gear, because the temperature plunged as they moved across the sky at three hundred plus knots an hour.

# Chapter 17

That the ground crew was having trouble was an understatement. The winds were blowing and swirling hard enough that the de-icing fluid would not stay on the wings long enough to work. The heated leading wing edges finally warmed up enough so that they could get the plane ready. The fuel personnel struggled to stay on their feet as they filled the plane with a full load of jet fuel. After fighting with the half-frozen fuel cap for twenty minutes, the ground crew finally got it in place. Two hours after the plane was scheduled to take off, the pilot motioned to Becca and Pam that it was time to depart. Bundling up once again, the two ladies made a dash across the tarmac and into the plane. The King Air was still warm inside, even though it had lost most of its heat while being de-iced, so Pam and Becca both elected to take their winter coats off. The plane started without incident and in five minutes was rolling down the runway for takeoff. That changed as soon as the plane was airborne, the landing gear was raised and it was as if they were on a roller coaster, the winds bounced the plane up and down. The pilot took the aircraft to eighteen thousand feet to try to smooth the ride, but to no avail.

The jostling and bumping had been going on for about an hour and both Pam and Becca were doing their best not to lose what little breakfast they had eaten. Each had their seatbelts pulled snugly against their waists and were holding tightly onto the arms of the seats. The turbulence suddenly subsided and the jet leveled out. Pam took a deep breath and looked over at Becca.

"I wasn't sure I could take much more of that," Pam said. "That bagel was doing its best to make a reappearance."

"I know what you mean," Becca concurred. "I was beginning to think my morning coffee was still perking."

"Maybe we can get a little sleep and recover from our trip to Six Flags over Canada," Pam said with a smile. She had barely finished speaking than the plane did a quick drop of about one hundred feet and then rose about seventy five feet.

"So much for our smooth ride home. Sorry," Pam apologized.

They both read of large chunks of ice falling to the ground, but neither was ready for the sound that one made hitting an aircraft at eighteen thousand feet in the air. A gunshot seemed quiet compared to the one that hit the fuselage of the Beechcraft King Air. Fortunately it just dented the plane's aluminum skin, but as the ice bounced off into the atmosphere it hooked the jet's antenna and knocked it into oblivion. Simultaneously, Becca and Pam tightened their seatbelts and grabbed their coats, a move that would save their lives.

Fifteen minutes later, a second more deadly piece of ice struck the turboprop jet, this one hit with the deadly accuracy of a World War II anti-aircraft gunner on the shores of England. The one hundred pound mass of frozen water falling at terminal velocity punched a hole two feet in diameter in the port wing, slicing through the fuel tank and spraying debris in all directions. A chunk of wing hit the port propeller knocking a section into the turbines. The ensuing explosion ripped the engine loose from its mounts leaving the plane with just a stub of a port wing.

Desperately the pilot, Mike Logan, fought to keep the plane aloft, but the downward force of the ice hitting the wing and then the loss of an engine had sent the craft into a death spiral. Logan cut back the power to the starboard engine and yanked the rudder hard to the right, this slowed the tight spiral a little and pulling the yoke back got the nose back up but they were still falling quickly.

"We are going down, hold on!" Mike called back to the passengers. He looked at the altimeter, its hands spinning like a fan in reverse indicating the speed of the jet's descent. Mentally Mike ran through the emergency checklist and counted down the feet.

*Seven thousand feet, start fuel dump, probably won't empty but might avoid explosion. Six thousand, no radio? Punch emergency beacon! Four thousand, we aren't slowing down, can't see crap out of the window, hope I am not over a lake. Should be over Superior National Forest, the middle of nowhere and freezing cold.*

*Two thousand, there was an opening in the clouds, a clearing pull hard. No landing gear, belly land, nose up hard, here we go.*

The plane hit hard, but fortunately was swinging around in the direction it was descending so it did not tumble and roll. Instead, it slid across frozen ground. For an instant, Mike Logan thought he had pulled off a miracle, then the starboard wing hit a large pine and swung the plane around, another large tree sheared off the tail section causing the plane to veer back around. The last thing that Chief Pilot Mike Logan saw was the large trunk of a spruce tree barreling at him, in vain he threw up his hands to protect his face, he silently prayed for his passengers and then darkness consumed him.

Kilkenny broke the silence about ten minutes into the flight. "The gunner says it is a two hour flight to the nearest airport. Murphy, maybe now would be a good time to brief us on what you have found out and what kind of a wild-ass plan you two NCOs have come up with."

Murphy smiled and pulled out the maps. "I managed to get a hold of the Fed's and found out what they know. They were none too happy about a boyfriend trying to play John Wayne and be a hero," Murphy shot a grin at Curtis and then continued, "Of course I didn't let them know that it was a boyfriend and four Marines coming up either. Anyway, as near as the Fed's have been able to pinpoint, the plane went down in this area about twenty miles from the border.

That in itself normally would not present a problem, we could just do a low level insert and walk out. But there are high winds and a snowstorm in the area and visibility is not good."

"So how close can we get?" Curtis inquired.

"Looks like we will have to land about fifteen miles from the edge of the search area at this small strip right here. Washington has been doing some of the initial planning from there on."

Gunny Washington took over at that point. "I made a couple calls to the reserve units up in this area to see if any of them had done any training in this part of the country, but none had. I finally talked to the S2 at the $5^{th}$ Recon in Duluth and he said that his gunny was an avid hiker and hunter and had been in the area last summer. Unfortunately he's at Disney with his family; the major did have his cell phone number and gave it to me. A couple of tries and bingo, Gunnery Sgt. Anderson was telling me all about the back country while waiting in line for the Magic Kingdom. Ain't technology grand?"

"OK, OK, we get the point," Curtis interrupted. "What did he have to say?"

"Patience, Colonel, patience. Anyway as I was saying, this gunny was up there last summer and was able give me a pretty good idea of the terrain. He says it is rough, tree-covered and he doubted that we could land a bird anywhere in the area. But he was pretty sure that we would be able to get within a couple of miles of the site by driving a Hummer in. The problem will be the two-mile or so hike to the scene, with the ruggedness of the terrain it would be all too easy to get separated and lost. The First Sergeant and myself put together a solution to that problem and also to the problem of getting back out together." The gunny handed each of the team two small pieces of electronics, each about the size of a walkman. "The one unit is the latest in GPS. We can use it to keep our location relative to each other and also to the plane and the Hummer. They are interlinked so each one has its own unique signature on the display. The comm unit is good for about five miles, is voice-activated and hands-free. Both pieces have batteries designed to stay charged in subzero weather. That brings us to the transportation problem, and once again the S2 came through for us. He has agreed to loan as part of the 'exercise' one of his HMMV's to use, along with a driver. He will meet us at Chisholm-Hibbling Airport when we land. Hopefully the NTSB will find the aircraft before we get there. Any questions?"

No one had any questions; each knew what they had to do and how to do it. One by one, they each leaned back and closed their eyes. Their minds rehearsed the mission and the problems, but their bodies rested. About thirty minutes out of Chisholm-Hibbling, Ramirez came over the intercom to wake them. Kilkenny reached over and put his hand on Curtis' leg, knocking back the headsets; he spoke so only the two could hear.

"Roy, you know that we are with you to the end on this." John spoke not as the CO but as a friend, "but are you prepared for the fact that she may be dead?"

"Yes, sir, I am," Curtis answered, "but I also know that I must bring her home one way or another." Curtis could feel the wind and snow beat on the side of the Sea Stallion. Looking out the window he could see nothing but a wall of snow. As the winds increased, the warrant officer radioed back to Kilkenny.

"Sir, if this wind gets much stronger we will be lucky to make into Chisholm in one piece. The tower says it is a total whiteout to the north. The NTSB has grounded all search aircraft and is ordering us to land."

"OK, set her down at Chisholm; I was hoping we could fly straight in but it looks like time for plan B."

"Aye, sir," he said and the bird swung over to the west on a course for Chisholm-Hibbling Airport. Visibility was almost zero by the time they landed and Chief Warrant Officer Ramirez was privately glad that he was not going to have to fly in this weather. The giant helicopter landed hard as Ramirez fought the winds. No sooner had the rotor blades started to slow than the four in the rear had disembarked and were headed for the terminal. Washington noticed the HMMV in the parking lot, so he knew at least they wouldn't have to walk all the way. The Marines were cold after the one hundred yard walk to the terminal and each wondered if they were ready for a two-mile march in this weather.

# Chapter 18

Richard Grassbaugh was not having a good day. He had been looking forward to leaving for Nashville with his wife for a short vacation. Instead here he was in the middle of a blizzard in the middle of nowhere with an airplane down in the woods and then to compound the problems, the boyfriend one of the passengers was on his way up here to play hero and rescue her. As the regional head of the NTSB, he planned to do everything within his power to keep this John Wayne wannabe grounded and out of his way. If that meant placing him under arrest, so be it.

The best estimate that his people could come up with, was that it was going to be at least 36 hours before the weather was fit to do an aerial search. So far they had received nothing in the way of emergency beacons or radio transmissions. This fact in itself made the possibility of survivors slim and when you added in the snow and the minus thirty degrees chill factor the odds got even slimmer. Grassbaugh did not like to write any downed aircraft as a complete loss, but it looked like this might be one of those times.

Grassbaugh was staring out the terminal window, wondering how this boyfriend was even going to make it to Chisholm let alone conduct a heroic search, when he spotted lights about a quarter mile to the south. They were coming in low and fast and by the steady whop, whop of the rotor blades he could tell that it was a helicopter. Who would be foolish enough to fly one in this weather? Well he would soon find out, that is, provided the pilot got the bird landed safely.

"Excuse me, sir."

"Yes?" Richard turned to see who had spoken to him. It was one of the technicians, Bryant Robinson, who knew more about computers and electronics than Grassbaugh ever would.

"Excuse me, sir, but I think you need to hear this." The young technician pointed back toward the bank of radios and scanners that they had sent up not two hours before. "It started about ten minutes ago and fades in and out."

Richard put the headphones on and listened carefully. Sure enough there was the faint but distinct sound of a black box homing beacon. They were fortunate that this King Air had had one installed. Regulations didn't require it for another year. Grassbaugh looked at his team and Bryant just nodded at him.

"I take it you have a fix on the aircraft," Grassbaugh asked. "Though I am not sure how you could, with as faint signal as you have."

"It wasn't easy," the skinny computer tech grinned, "but with a little help from the GPS system, I think we are within two hundred yards or so."

"In this weather that might not be close enough. Show me on the map where you have it marked."

"It is charted on this map." The huge regional map was crisscrossed with lines and circles and centering on an area about fifteen miles northeast of the airport in the middle of Superior National Forest. Grassbaugh just shook his head as he stared at the map. The topographical markings showed the location to be one of the most rugged in northern Minnesota. It was full of ridges and ravines and it would be difficult even in calm weather to land a rescue helicopter in that area. Couldn't he just once, he wished, get a break? His thoughts were interrupted by the sound of the winter wind howling as the door from the tarmac opened. Grassbaugh noticed that the chopper had landed safely and made a mental note to find out what fool had been piloting it.

With the opening of the door came four men in from the cold. They could only be described as four polar bears, their white parkas added to the bulkiness of the already large men. Grassbaugh observed that they were military and that at least two were officers. *What would bring Marines to this part of the world?* he wondered. The four men made their way directly over to where he was standing.

"Excuse me," the colonel began, "could you tell me who is in charge of the crash investigation?"

"That would be me," Grassbaugh responded, "Richard Grassbaugh, Senior Investigator, NTSB. What can I do for you, Colonel?"

"Colonel John Kilkenny, we are from the Marine Reserve Battalion in Chicago and we are here to assist in the rescue operation anyway possible."

"Why would Marines be interested in, oh I get it now, you're the boyfriend," Grassbaugh said with a smile that bordered on being a smirk.

"No, sir, the Lt. Colonel over there is the John Wayne boyfriend, but all of us know the passengers and we mean to bring them in one way or another," Kilkenny said in a tone that left little doubt that he was in charge.

"OK, the weather is terrible and I am not sending any of my personnel out there. If you want to kill yourselves being heroes go right ahead," Grassbaugh replied.

"Well, that's what Marines do, die heroes. Now if you will be so kind as to show Gunnery Sergeant Washington anything you have in the way of location and terrain information, the rest of us will see to our gear." The door to the parking lot opened and another young corporal in winter gear walked in.

"Sir, Corporal Roger McCoy reporting as ordered with one HMMV at your disposal," the Marine said, coming to attention. "As always, the Major sends his compliments and says if you need any other gear or men I am to let him know."

"Thank you, Corporal. At ease." Kilkenny introduced the rest of the men. "This is First Sergeant Murphy, Gunnery Sergeant Washington is over there by the maps, CWO4 Ramirez is piloting the chopper and this is Lt. Colonel Curtis, he is the reason we are on this mission, it is his lady that is a passenger of the plane. Now since time is of paramount importance, get the HMMV over to the helicopter and help the gunner transfer our gear."

"Aye, sir," McCoy acknowledged, turned and headed out the door.

"OK, let's see what Washington has found out," Kilkenny replied.

Washington was coming over from the wall map, shaking his head. "It's doable, but it is going to be tough. The NTSB has a fix within 200 yards, but in this weather you could be twenty feet away and miss it. I got the GPS coordinates and I'll program them into the units while we head out. We should be able to get within two miles but it will take probably one and a half to two hours to cover the remaining ground."

"If the Hummer is loaded, let's not waste any more time. Load 'em up," Kilkenny ordered. The four Marines headed out the door and back out on to the tarmac. The temperature felt like it had dropped another five degrees and each knew it was going to get worse before it got better. Corporal McCoy was waiting in the HMMV when the rest arrived. McCoy spoke as the rest buckled up.

"Sir, the gunner said he would stay by the radio in case we needed an airlift. Also I only see four sets of gear, am I not going in with you?"

"Corporal, this wild mission is not your affair, but it is ours. What I need you to do is to keep this machine running and warm so that when we get back we will be able to beat it to a hospital if need be. Understand, Marine?"

"Understood, sir. Where to, sir?"

"The gunny has the map," Kilkenny replied. Following the route that the guys from the NTSB had laid out it looked like it would be about fifteen miles by HMMV until the road disappeared and then another two miles on foot. Curtis hoped that they had done their calculations correctly or else it was going to be a long night.

Three minutes after they left the airfield, Curtis knew that the going would be extra tough. Besides the thermometer dropping, the wind had increased in speed and was blowing snow. Visibility was next to nothing and McCoy was fighting to see the road. A half hour later, they turned onto the logging trail for the last miles of this leg. The only way they kept going was that there were no trees in front of them and the HMMV had high clearance. Twice they were jolted as the vehicle crossed fallen trees that were hidden by the snow. Corporal McCoy suddenly slammed the brakes as they rounded the corner. The road had just ended, trees blocked forward and left, on the right the edge slipped away almost vertical, down a thirty-foot cliff.

Roy was the first out, had the back door opened, and was getting his gear out before the rest started to move. Each man carried a thirty-pound pack loaded with medical supplies and emergency rations. They also carried ropes and a take-apart stretcher/sled. In all, their gear weighed close to sixty pounds each. Curtis tested his radio and GPS, double-checking that the location of the HMMV was properly locked in. Each Marine checked the other's pack to make sure it was strapped in properly.

"Let's go, we are burning daylight," Roy said, turning on his flashlight. The others smiled grimly, but said nothing; they knew that daylight was long gone and that anybody that had been in this kind of weather for as long as crash victims had it was unlikely that they would be alive. Following the GPS readings, Lt. Colonel Roy Curtis stepped out into the darkness with his friends behind him. It only took a few yards before Curtis realized how tough this trek was really going to be. If the GPS said it was going to be two miles as the crow flies, then the actual hike would be more like three miles. They immediately started down a steep descent and then were met immediately with a climb that was every bit as high.

The snow continued to blow and visibility decreased to a few yards. The original idea of spreading out and covering a wider search area was abandoned, because if a mishap were to occur they would not be able to find each other. Guided by the blinking light on his GPS, doggedly Roy pushed on. The red light on the small screen had come to represent Becca's red hair and the fire that burned in his heart for her. As they trudged slowly up and down the ravines, Roy thought of Becca and the times they had had together. Of their first meeting at the art exhibition and the time they had spent at Christmas time with the sleigh ride. Good times and some not-so-good, but great memories anyway. Just when he would begin to tire or get cold one of those memories would spur him on harder.

Finally at the end of the first hour, they were only about halfway there. Colonel Kilkenny touched Curtis's arm. "We have to stop and rest for a minute. If we don't, we won't have the strength to bring them out."

"OK, we will stop at the bottom of the next ravine, when we are out of the wind a little," Curtis reluctantly agreed. Carefully they made their way down the side of the ravine. Murphy led the way to a small group of trees, where the four searchers stopped. Washington unfolded a tarp and the men sat down to rest. Kilkenny handed hand warmers to each of them and they inserted them into their gloves. A warm fire could not have felt any better as the heat from the chemical reactions warmed their hands and blood.

"See if you can raise McCoy on the radio," Kilkenny suggested to Washington. The big Marine nodded, pulled the radio from his belt and keyed the mike.

"This is Marine Search One calling Marine Search Two." The reply came almost immediately.

"Marine Search Two, go ahead, One." The answer was full of static but understandable.

"Hey, McCoy, we are in a ravine about halfway there. It is blowing hard and slow going."

"No sign of it letting up here either. The NTSB called and wanted info. I told them no news is good news."

"Good job, keep the engine running. We will be home soon. Marine Search One out."

"Marine Search Two out. Semper Fi."

"Semper Fi." Washington slid the radio back in its pouch and stood to go. Curtis handed him an energy bar and a cup of warm coffee to drink while the First Sergeant packed away his ground tarp. The coffee warmed the insides of the gunny's body and the energy bar just plain tasted good. Refreshed and reloaded, the four picked the trail up and over the next hill.

Roy looked at his watch the time was twenty-two hundred hours. It had been almost ten hours since the plane had probably crashed. Ten hours in sub-zero weather, with little, if any, shelter and probably injured also. As despair shot through his body, it seemed to drain the very life source from him. He knew that the only hope of saving Becca and the rest lay with the four of them, so drawing on every last bit of will he plunged on. The others, sensing his strength, followed their friend once again into the darkness.

# Chapter 19

A cold wind blew across Becca's face, the ice stung her cheeks and like a light slap, they revived her to consciousness. Slowly she awoke and remembered what had happened. The chunk of ice hitting the plane, she and Pam grabbing their coats, the spin, the crash, then blackness. Opening her eyes, she looked around seeing pieces of what had been the plane were strewn as far as she could she see. Realizing that she was still buckled into her seat, Becca reached up to unfasten her seatbelt. The motion stopped suddenly as pain shot through her right arm and shoulder. Carefully, Becca took inventory of the rest of her body and miraculously, aside from a couple of scratches and bruises, she had no other broken bones. Left-handed, Becca released the seatbelt and stood up, her right arm hanging limply at her side.

"Where was Pam?" she thought aloud. "Did she survive? How about the pilot?" Looking around she spied Pam's seat laying on its side about ten yards away, slowly she stumbled over to it. The seat was facing away and as she approached, Becca heard the moaning of an injured person. Pam was hurt but still alive.

"Pam? Pam!" Becca called as she ran to her assistant and friend. "Are you OK? What's hurt?"

"I think my left leg is broken," Pam cried back as Becca leaned in and unbuckled her. She noticed a large gash on Pam's forehead but didn't say anything about it.

"Let's get you up and find some shelter, the wind is picking up," Becca said. Helping Pam up, Becca helped her hop over to a tree and then leaned her against it. "Hang on, I'll drag your seat over for you to sit in."

One-armed, Becca struggled to get the aircraft seat into an upright position and pushed it over to the tree, helping Pam back down in it. She stuck her hands in her pockets to warm them and felt the cold steel of the multi-tool that Roy had given her to use around the farm. She had carried it as a memento and now it would serve its function.

"Gibson, catch." Becca tossed the tool to Gibson. "Cut me off a piece of seatbelt and help me make a sling." Nodding, Pam reached down and sliced through the seatbelt. Carefully she helped Becca bring her arm up and tie the strap around her neck. Becca cut the other strap off and taking a couple of small branches fashioned a set of splints for Pam's leg. Pam secured the strap around the splints holding her leg stiff.

"Becca, I am getting cold," Pam said. "We need to find some shelter."

"Hang in there. I'll see if I can find anything to make a shelter and fire." Becca stood up and felt the wind and snow hit her face once again. Most of the wreckage was scattered to the north, so she headed up the line of wreckage. One hundred yards up the line; Becca found what she was looking for. The starboard wing tip was wedged against two trees forming a wall. Ducking down beside the wing she got out of the wind long enough to get the circulation going again, then getting up she headed back to Pam. Hooking Pam's arm over her shoulder; Becca helped Pam to the wing. Becca dragged a couple more pieces of fuselage over to Pam and with her help got a halfway decent lean-to made.

The wind was continuing to pick up speed and the ice was beginning to feel like needles as they hit Becca's face. She picked up small sticks and scraps of magazines scattered around the crash site. Now if she could just get a fire going, she hoped that all this teaching on Indians would pay off.

"Becca, are we going to make it?"

"I think so. I am getting cold too."

"Will they find us?" Real doubts were beginning to creep into Pam's mind.

"Roy will find us, I know he will." Somehow the thought of Roy coming for her boosted her strength. Yes, Roy would come for her. It would daylight for a couple of more hours and then it would get really cold. She remembered seeing the tail section a little to the north; maybe the emergency bag was nearby. She stumbled north toward the area where the tail section should be, another fifty yards she found what was left of the emergency bag. Becca rummaged through the bag and found what she was looking for, a part of a flare with the igniter attached. Warmth assured, she headed back to the lean-to. Visibility was getting worse and Becca almost walked right by the wing.

Pam was shivering and her teeth were chattering when Becca returned. Pam had formed a teepee of wood and tinder. Becca didn't realize how cold she was until she tried to start the flare. After half a dozen tries, the flare took and started to burn. Laying the burning flare at the base of the wooden teepee, slowly the fire took hold and soon a nice warm fire was burning. Becca and Pam huddled over the fire and gradually the frost left their bodies.

"We have a little light left, I am going to try and find the pilot and maybe a little food," Becca said. "Will you be OK?"

"I should be; my leg is too numb to hurt. Please hurry, I don't want to be here alone."

"Twenty minutes max, it is getting too cold out there." Becca slipped out of the lean-to and into the arctic air once again. She headed down the wreckage trail and soon stumbled onto the cockpit wrapped around the base of a tree. Becca could make out the outline of a body pinned in the cockpit. It was obvious to her that the pilot was dead so she headed back to the lean-to, gathering pieces of wood in her good arm as she went. Halfway back to the shelter, she found a cushion from the cabin couch. Loading the wood onto the cushion, she started to drag it back when she spied her travel bag. Placing it on the pad she finished dragging it back.

"Good news, Pam," Becca said as she poked her head into the shelter. Pam was curled up trying to stay warm. "Here, sit on this, and look what I found," she said, holding up her travel bag.

"Great, we have makeup," Pam said sarcastically as she crawled onto the cushion.

"No, goofy, food. A large bag of M&M's to be exact." Becca tossed the bag of candy to Pam and curled up beside her. "Well, we have heat and food, so now all we have to do is wait on my knight to come rescue us."

Pam inquired again, "You really think he will come?"

"If I have learned anything about Roy Curtis in the last nine months, it's that it will take more than a blizzard to stop him. Pass the candy, please."

It was turning dark and the icy wind continued to blow, snow was piling up around their refuge; this was a mixed blessing as it acted as insulation blocking out the wind, but it would make them harder to find. The aluminum fuselage pieces reflected the heat and the sanctuary was fairly comfortable. Becca had stockpiled enough wood to last the night if they kept the fire small. Snuggling as closely as they could, they prepared to wait out the storm until help arrived.

The second leg was not much easier than the first, but just a little. The trees were just as dense but the ground was a little flatter and the squad made better time. One step after another they trudged on. Slowly the lights on the GPS units moved closer together. The squad was about a quarter of a mile from the crash area when they stumbled into a clearing. It was only about two hundred feet in diameter but large enough to land the helicopter when the weather broke. Instinctively each member of the team locked the GPS reading into their units. None of them wanted to make the trek back to the HMMV if they didn't have to. The wind slackened as they reached the far side of the clearing, visibility seemed to increase and Roy thought he could see a small light to the northeast about three hundred yards away.

"Colonel Curtis, look to your right about two o'clock. I think I see a light, it appears to be a small fire." The voice crackled in Curtis' headset, startling him. They had been concentrating so hard on walking through the blizzard that no one had thought of speaking.

"I just saw it, First Sergeant, thanks," Curtis replied, and with all his remaining strength, he hurried toward the small fire. Branches tore at his face and clothes as he plowed through the underbrush, but Roy didn't feel any pain he only focused on the glow ahead. If there was a controlled fire, then there was a chance that someone might still be alive. An Olympic sprinter never ran the last two hundred yards harder than Roy did, leaving the other three far behind. Roy could make out a pile of plane pieces with two figures huddled underneath it near the glowing flames. One of them, a woman, screamed hysterically as Roy entered into the area lit up by the fire. He ignored the screaming woman and instead dropped his pack and took the other woman in his arms. Stiff from the cold, Becca reached up and buried her face into his coat and cried.

By this time the other three men had reached the fire and quickly each dropped his pack and opened it. Murphy and Washington came over with their medical kits to look over the women while Kilkenny set about rigging some tarps to increase the size of the shelter. Aside from her broken leg, which Washington put in an air cast, Pam was fine except for a little frostbite on her ears and cheeks. Roy let go of Becca long enough for Murphy to examine her. Her cheeks didn't show any signs of frostbite; Roy helped Murphy immobilize her arm with a splint.

"No chance of getting back out tonight, sir," Washington informed Colonel Kilkenny. "Also, we are having trouble getting through to either the gunner or to Corporal McCoy at the truck. I think it is because the wind has picked up speed again and the snow is interfering with the transmission."

"Thanks, First Sergeant. OK, let's make these ladies comfortable and then hunker down until daylight," Kilkenny informed the other three rescuers. "Curtis, do you think you can break away long enough to get some chow cooked?"

Curtis, who had been holding Becca tight inside a thermal blanket, looked at her and she gave him the "I'll be OK for a minute" smile, so he tucked the blanket tightly around her and got up to make some food.

"Colonel," Roy asked in his signature smart-aleck tone, "do you want your prime rib rare or well done?"

"Well, I see the stress of the moment is over," Kilkenny chuckled. "Just fix me some eggs over well and shut up."

"Wishes, wishes, wishes," Roy muttered good naturedly. "I give a guy prime rib and he wants eggs." Curtis opened the pack and took out packets of dehydrated food and began to prepare them. The aroma of the stew that was being cooked soon filled the air and the two women who had just minutes before had worried about whether they would survive the night, now only wondered if supper was about ready.

"It's not Delmonico's but it is warm," Curtis said as he handed Becca her plate.

"I won't complain, but I'll take Delmonico's next week." Becca weakly smiled as she spoke. The food warmed her body from deep within and she could feel life begin to surge back through her.

"Marine Search Two to Marine Search One, come in, One." The radio suddenly crackled to life, causing everyone to jump at the noise.

"Go ahead Two, this is One," Gunnery Sergeant Washington answered.

"Sir, I am sorry but the NTSB called half an hour ago and said that if you didn't make contact within fifteen minutes you were to return. I have been trying to reach you ever since," Corporal McCoy apologized.

"McCoy," Kilkenny took the radio away from the gunny and said, "this is Colonel Kilkenny. You call those impatient snobs back and tell them the Marines have accomplished the mission and there are two, I repeat two, survivors, no serious injuries, and we will call in first thing in the morning. After you have delivered the message, you are to shut down the radio, stay warm, and sleep until morning then head back to the airport. I will radio Ramirez in the a.m. with instructions. Understood?"

"Understood, sir," came the reply. "May I be so bold to ask if the Lt. Colonel's lady is among the survivors?"

"Yes, you may ask," Kilkenny looked over at his friends, "and the answer is yes, now get some sleep."

"Thank you, sir. Marine Search Two out. Semper Fi." Then the radio went dead.

Though only temporary, the shelter kept the wind and snow off of them. Kilkenny had rigged the tarps so that air would circulate, but the snow would not enter. This allowed them to keep the fire going and heat the area to above freezing. The wind continued to blow and snow piled up against the sides of the structure. After eating, Roy checked on Becca, her hands had not been frozen, but they now were starting to hurt as they began to warm up. Gently Roy took each hand and held it between his until they had warmed, a tear formed on Becca's cheek as the pain in her hands subsided. Roy sat down beside her and wrapped his big parka around her shoulders and held her tight.

"I was so afraid that I wouldn't be able to find you in time," he said, fighting back the tears. "I don't know if I could have gone on without you. I need you so much."

"I knew you would come," Becca said with confidence. "I was sure that my cowboy would come to my rescue once again and you can ask Pam, because I told her you would. It was just a matter of holding on long enough."

"You had more confidence in me than I did. How about you leaning against your cowboy and getting some rest." Roy pulled her tight against his side and held her. After just a few minutes, both had drifted off to sleep as the sounds of the night winds sang them a lullaby.

With the first rays of light, the rescuers started to move. The storm had passed and drifts of snow were piled high. Colonel Kilkenny set about making a quick, hot breakfast and coffee, while the Gunnery Sergeant Washington checked on his two patients. With the skies clear, it was easy for Murphy to contact Ramirez and Corporal McCoy. The Corporal was already on his way back to the airport and the gunner said that he would be at the landing site in about one hour.

Gently, Roy woke Becca. She had hardly moved since she had fallen asleep the evening before. Stiffly she moved and stretched, wincing in pain once when she bumped her arm against the tree they had been leaning on, but otherwise she seemed fine. Roy kissed her lightly on the lips as he helped her up. Once he was sure she was OK, Roy decided to do a little exploring while breakfast was cooking.

Kicking the tarps open, Curtis had to dig his way through the snowdrift to get out. Even with snowshoes on, Curtis and Murphy sank deeply into the snow. Slowly they surveyed the crash site as they headed toward the cockpit of the downed aircraft, they both stopped and stared. The turboprop aircraft was scattered over several hundred square yards, the pieces of the main fuselage were stuck into two large trees, and the rest of the starboard wing had sheared off and was sticking up out of the snow one hundred feet behind it. As they approached from the rear, they could smell the jet fuel as it dripped from the wing tanks. Becca and Pam had been lucky that the plane had not gone up in flames when the wings were ripped away. Carefully the two Marines picked their way through the tangled wreckage until they reached what was left of the rear cabin. Somehow the ladies had landed on the outside; the two seatbacks that they had been seated in could just barely be seen sticking out of the drifted snow. Ed stuck his head inside and took a quick look around.

"I don't know how they survived, sir," the First Sergeant commented, shaking his head as he backed away from the door. "There is gear and seats thrown everywhere. I bet it was one helluva ride. Let's head up front, I didn't see any signs of the pilot."

"Pam told the gunny that he was dead in the cockpit," Curtis told him. "Becca confirmed it and said that she couldn't get to him with only one arm and all they were worried about was staying alive until help came."

"If the cockpit is not where the snow was blown clear, we probably won't find him."

"Yeah I know, but I hate the thought of leaving anyone here."

The two of them spread apart about twenty feet and began the search for the lost pilot. The cockpit had broken away from the cabin area and was in bits and pieces throughout the brush. The snow wasn't deep here but if you didn't stumble on him you could walk right by and not see the body. Curtis looked at his watch and was just about to call off the search when Murphy shouted.

"Over here, Colonel," the First Sergeant waved. "I think I am going to need a little help."

"On my way!" Roy hollered back as he waded through the deep drift that separated the two. There wedged against the tree was the cockpit and the remains of the pilot. From the angle of his head it was fairly obvious he had a broken neck and had died quickly. It took a lot of tugging and prying with their walking poles, but they finally got the body out of the cockpit. Taking out the body bag he had been carrying, Murphy positioned it by the body. Quickly and carefully they put the stiff body of Chief Pilot Mike Logan into the body bag and began the short journey back to the shelter.

Becca and Pam were sitting in two of the collapsible sleds that the team had brought with them. Both were looking much better than they had been the previous night. Roy leaned over and gave Becca a long kiss before he spoke.

"You are looking much better, sugar. John's cooking must be extra good today."

"That and a little of Jack Daniel's brew," Becca replied. Isaiah Washington just grinned and turned away. Roy Curtis shook his head and laughed.

"Colonel Kilkenny," Murphy said, "Warrant Officer Ramirez says he is airborne and twenty minutes out. We need to get going."

"All right, gentlemen...." Colonel Kilkenny started to give the command but was interrupted by Lt. Colonel Curtis.

"Excuse me, sir," Curtis began. "I was supposed to do this last night at dinner at your house and I don't want to wait another minute."

Turning to Becca he knelt own on one knee. "Rebecca Davidson, nine months ago I told you that you looked great in the moonlight and today in the morning light you look absolutely radiant."

Tears flowed from Becca's eyes as she realized what Roy was doing and her hand covered her mouth as sobs of joy tried to escape.

"What I am trying to say is," Roy once again was speechless and struggling to find the right words, "will you marry me?"

"Yes," was all Becca could say as she held her man tightly among the cheers from the others.

"Gentlemen," Kilkenny began again, "and ladies, now that the ceremonies are all finished, you heard the First Sergeant, let's saddle up and move out. Curtis, I assume you are pulling one of the sleds, Washington, you take the other lady. The First Sergeant and I will bring the third and the extra gear. Let's move out."

"Aye, sir!!" the three Marines shouted in unison. Though the load was heavier than on the way in, the burden on Curtis' heart was much lighter and the others had to hustle to keep up. They reached the clearing and Kilkenny tossed a colored smoke marker into the middle so that Ramirez could see them and tell the wind direction. As soon as the blades began to slow, they headed toward the side door of the helicopter. In less than five minutes the ladies and the rescuers were loaded. The pilot's body was loaded into the far aft and they were off. The flight back to Chisholm-Hibbling airport was a quick one now that the winds had died down. In fifteen minutes, they settled the big helicopter onto the tarmac and were loading the injured and dead in awaiting ambulances.

"Curtis," Colonel Kilkenny said as the paramedics started to close the doors on the ambulances, "you go with her and we will take care on everything else."

"Aye, sir," Curtis turned as he entered the ambulance, "and thank you, sir."

"Semper Fi."

"Semper Fi, sir."

The ride to the hospital was totally uneventful. Becca and Pam, both exhausted and now warm, fell asleep. Awakened only long enough to be examined, treated, and transferred to warm beds the two ladies spent the rest of the day and night asleep.

When Becca awoke in the morning she was surprised to see all four of her rescuers sitting in the room. Pam was already awake and was talking to Chris. Ramirez had relayed the news of the rescue to the university and they had called Chris. He had driven all night and had reached the hospital shortly after they had been transferred to their room. Isaiah had a Sharpie pen and was signing Pam's leg cast. There were flowers everywhere; Becca leaned back and inhaled deeply, the fragrance of the flowers filling her lungs. Roy got out of the chair he was sitting and took her hand.

"Good morning, sunshine." He kissed her lightly on the lips. "Are you feeling better?"

"I am feeling much better, thank you." She looked at the rest of the men, including Ramirez and McCoy, who were coming through the door. "I don't know how to begin to thank all of you for saving us."

"No thanks needed, ma'am," Colonel John Patrick Kilkenny said, trying to sound military-like, "just one thing though."

"What is that?" Becca asked with a slightly puzzled look on her face.

"Just love that cowboy and make him happy." A huge smile broke across John's face.

"That I can do," she said, hooking her good arm around Roy's neck and planting a huge kiss on him.

Printed in the United Kingdom by
Lightning Source UK Ltd., Milton Keynes
139864UK00001B/93/A